BREADWINNER

The Weight of Blood and Bread

*To Charlotte
With love
from Mum*

Eucharia Udie

*4/5/25
The Author ♡*

Conscious Dreams
PUBLISHING

Breadwinner. The Weight of Blood and Bread

Copyright ©2024: Eucharia Udie

All rights reserved. No part of this publication may be produced, distributed, or transmitted in photocopying, recording, or other electronic or mechanical methods, any form or by any means, including without the prior written permission of the publisher, except in the case of brief quotations embodied in critical reviews and certain other non-commercial uses permitted by copyright law.

This is a work of fiction. Names, characters, businesses, places, events and incidents are either the products of the author's imagination or used in a fictitious manner. Any resemblance to actual persons, living or dead, or actual events is purely coincidental.

First Printed in United Kingdom, 2024

Published by Conscious Dreams Publishing
www.consciousdreamspublishing.com

Edited by Elise Abram

Typeset by Oksana Kosovan

ISBN: 978-1-917584-07-4

Dedication

For my Sterling Daughters—
Awhobiwom, Liyiaunim and Ushang.

Contents

About the Author 7

The Judgement 9

Hard Times 17

The Carnival 29

Farewell 45

Goodbye Lagos 53

The Great Change 75

A New Wife 85

A Larger Family 99

Jangilova — Epo-Motor 109

Breaking News 119

Stainless-Bobo 131

The Traditional Marriage 143

Giant Step 155

Greener Pastures 163

Bank Alert 175
The Phone Call 183
The Revelation 191
A Fresh Start.. 201
Milking the Cow 209
Once Upon a Christmas 219
Home At Last 231
An Adversity.. 245
Acknowledgments 253

About the Author

Eucharia Udie was born in 1994 to the family of Mr. and Mrs. Kinu Undiandeye. She earned a bachelor's degree in Mass Communication from Cross River University of Technology, Calabar, where she discovered her passion for creative writing and storytelling, developing expertise in utilizing diverse media techniques.

Her career journey reflects her versatility and dedication to continuous learning. She began as an intern reporter at Cross Broadcasting Corporation (CRBC), sharpening her investigative journalism and reporting skills. Later, she relocated to England, where she served as a healthcare assistant and a 999-emergency operator with British Telecom. Currently, Eucharia is an energy specialist with E.on Next, where she provides expert solutions in energy management and efficiency.

In addition to her professional endeavours, Eucharia is an avid writer, focusing on themes related to her Christian faith and the deeper conversations of life, which she shares to inspire and connect with her readers. She is also a food blogger, blending storytelling with digital photography to share her culinary creations.

Eucharia is married to Dr. Justin Udie and is the proud mother of three children, Awhobiwom, Liyiaunim, and Ushang.

The Judgement

As the morning sun rose above the bustling town of Yaba, Lagos State, Nigeria, the city came alive with the rhythmic harmony of its diverse inhabitants. Long dark shadows cast on both tarred and untarred roads moved with lightning speed. Strangers bumped into each other, rubbing sweat and inhaling breaths from unfamiliar faces. Men and women, once dressed in classy suits and ties, threw all formality out the window as they fought for space on rickety *danfo* buses.

The traders at the Tejousho Market bartered their goods by the roadside with raised voices. Some enticed customers to their shops with customized songs, while others pulled arms and gave far-from-truthful compliments.

The aroma of early morning street food mixed with muddy soil from previous rainfalls filled the air, and the sounds of children playing football at the market echoed in the streets.

Amidst this chaos, the Yaba Chief Magistrate Court stood firmly as a dispenser of justice. Within its walls, diverse people were integrated, each with their own struggles and peculiarities. Others hung outside the courtroom, seeking assistance from pro bono lawyers.

On that day, the courtroom buzzed with anticipation as an elderly southern Nigerian took his place in the dock. From his looks, he was probably in his early fifties, dressed in a typical Niger Delta *etibo* with trousers to match. In the centre of his navy-blue top were three silver buttons running vertically, with a thin silver chain connecting them. The silver chain curled to his left breast pocket, where another shiny button lay. This simple but unique Niger Delta costume was usually accompanied by a walking stick and felt hat, but out of respect for the court, the defendant left his bald head exposed to the audience gathered to witness his trial.

Within the hallowed court chambers, Judge Damian Okoro conducted the hearing of the case with solemn grace, his gaze unwavering as he sifted through the intricacies of the case before him. He looked at the defendant soberly, his round Coke-bottle glasses resting on the tip of his broad nose. Even though he had presided over several cases in the past three decades, the courtroom wonders never seemed to end.

The Judge delivered his verdict, counting his words and hearing himself speak as the heart of the court beat on, its pulse echoing through the hall with a weighty finality. The people held their breath, acutely aware of the gravity of the moment. In this melting pot of cultures, justice was not merely a concept but a tangible force, shaping the lives of all who passed through its doors.

"Mr Gregory Ipeh," the judge said, "based on the evidence presented before me today, this court finds you guilty on all charges levied against you. For this reason, you shall be dismissed from your job as a Nigerian railway officer without benefits, incur a fine of three hundred thousand *naira* and complete thirty hours of unpaid labour, cutting the grass around the railway station as a punishment for all you have caused the corporation. This should be a lesson to others that honesty remains the best policy. A good name is better than silver and gold." The honourable judge hit his gavel on the wooden gavel pad to conclude his ruling and began making his way out of the courtroom.

The bailiff's voice followed in the usual ritual: "Court!"

Everyone stood up, whispering indiscriminately as Judge Damian made his way to his private chambers.

The shock of the ruling was palpable, like a jolt of electricity surging through his body. Gregory began to shiver. The sweat on his forehead was so great that it hit the wooden table like drizzling rain. With sweaty palms and unsteady feet, he reached for the wooden chair behind him, embarrassed, confused, and remorseful all at the same time. For the first time since he was caught, the gravity of his crime hit him like a ton of bricks. When he'd committed the offence, it seemed smart to have schemed his way for many years unnoticed, not to mention the additional pay he got from it and the joy of being able to cheat for fun. Like one of those male mannequins in fashion store windows, Gregory sat there frozen in time, biting his lower lip in absolute disgust at his actions.

He tried to look around the courtroom, but all he saw were fleeting images of blurry faces moving past and whispering loudly. Some law students dressed in white T-shirts, black skirts, and trousers gathered at the back of the courtroom with writing materials, making reference to his case.

He prayed for the ground to open and swallow him up so he would be free from the eye daggers piercing into his soul. Some stared out of pity, shaking their heads with crossed arms, while others looked on in disgust at his workplace misconduct. One lady pulled on both of her ears whilst speaking to her son in a muffled tone. No one had to eavesdrop to know she was warning him of the consequences of bad choices.

Gregory accepted his fate. He had to move on. Thank God for his excellent lawyer and friend, Barrister Donatus, who'd pleaded his case. Many people had believed Gregory would spend a few years in jail, so even though he had shamefully lost his job of twenty-five years with no retirement benefits, there was something to be thankful for.

However, his days of working with the Nigerian Railway Corporation in Lagos as a ticket officer were over. The benefits of having discounted train tickets for members of staff, easy access to medical treatments, and grocery vouchers, amongst others, were the perks the company graciously offered its employees. Sadly, Gregory and a few others wanted more. They fished out desperate customers and sold them train tickets at a cheaper rate. These customers were later grouped and snuck onto the train using the staff-only entrance and exit. They were made to stand in the train's aisle for hours, hanging onto the rails for their safety. This activity, though strenuous, was a good deal for both the financially handicapped and the shady customers who paid chicken feed to the workplace poachers rather than going through the legal route of buying tickets. Now, in the twinkle of an eye, a good twenty-five years of service had gone down the drain, all thanks to the CCTV cameras launched by the new minister of transportation to serve as evidence when resolving customers' complaints of stolen goods and ill-treatment by staff, amongst other issues. However, the trap meant to catch the rat had entangled an antelope; one stone had targeted more than one bird.

A few other workers at the railway corporation who'd toed the same line of deceit understood what these new cameras were capable of doing and temporarily staved off illegal activities until they had mastered how to be more discreet with their crime of engaging in unethical practices. Still, Gregory had thrown caution to the wind, claiming that nobody checked the CCTV cameras. It was an action that had landed him in a hot pot of soup. He'd become the sole transgressor, caught red-handed by the ruthless CCTV cameras.

Why were strange faces without Identity cards using the staff-only exit and entrance, crouching like lizards on their bellies to access a public train? When they got into the train, why were the same passengers not properly seated but hanging in the corners of the train before tickets were issued to legitimate customers who were still waiting in a long queue? These questions helped uncover the profound revelation of the misdemeanours that had gone unchecked at the NRC for too long.

Gregory was observed for about a month before substantial evidence could be collated to aid the court trial.

As you would imagine, life became unbearable after paying the stipulated court fine. Gregory no longer had a job, and he was turned down everywhere he went to seek employment.

Unfortunately, employers in Lagos wouldn't hire him over the cluster of agile and able-bodied Millennials and Gen Zers in the labour market with clean slates seeking the same role.

His house rent was almost due, and he had no hope of a renewal. The thought of how his Lagos landlord might approach recovering his rent scared him to death. He thought about being locked out of his home with his family and nosy neighbours prying into his family affairs.

Also, his daughters' school fees had to be attended to or else, for the first time in their lives, they would be called out on the assembly ground and sent shamefully home to their parents on a fee drive until their school fees were paid.

What to do? What to do?

Gregory made the hard decision to relocate his family to Bebuagbong, his village home in Obudu, a rural area in Cross River State, Nigeria. The only issue was that he was one of those Lagosians who only knew how to earn and spend, so he didn't have enough money to renovate his village home. The Bebuagbong community in Lagos were gracious. They offered an emergency loan to help him put things in place and prepare to move his wife, Felicia, and their six daughters to start life afresh in the village. There, the cost of living was much more affordable than in the cosmopolitan city of Lagos.

Hard Times

Felicia didn't welcome the news of relocating to the village as exciting. Leaving the seasoned city of Lagos for their unrefined village in Obudu was like dropping from grace to grass. They would lose their pride and high-handedness and become regular people. She prayed her husband would find another job in Lagos and cancel the idea of relocating, but the odds were clearly against them.

Also, she forbade exposing her poor daughters to the harsher reality of life compared to the soft landing Lagos had offered them. She thought about forfeiting the food business she had built from scratch over many years and feared starting all over again in a new environment.

Felicia sat on the edge of their oak bed that night, pondering deeply about this, the sight of her jobless husband snoring away to glory infuriated her. Where have you ever seen a jobless man sleeping with his two eyes closed, she wondered as tears of frustration trickled down her bony cheeks. She pulled a string of slimy mucus making its way into her open mouth, gasped for air and rubbed her fingers on an old piece of rag that had been lying in the corner.

In the market where she sold *akara* (bean cake) and *ogi* (corn porridge), she had heard about nothing but her husband's gross misconduct at his workplace for weeks. When the troublemakers describing what had happened spoke in extreme exaggeration, they twisted their mouths to the side, pouting towards her to indicate whose husband it was that had shamefully lost everything he had due to his 'long throat'.

"If you know how much of government money that man thief, you go sorry for the Nigerian people," one woman had said in pidgin English, backing Felicia's shop with her mountainous *ikebe* (bottom). She was Big Mama T, a business competitor who sold the same akara and ogi meal a few shops away, only that she had started her business many years before Felicia had begun to gather customers from around the area. This was a new development that had unsettled Big Mama T to the point where she once spread a rumour about Felicia using *juju* (charm) to attract customers. Hence, the long queue trooping into her shop daily asking for second rounds of delicious akara and licking their sticky fingers after scraping their ogi bowls. Big Mama T wondered why her regular customers had ditched her meals for Felicia's, and they only came to her shop after Felicia had exhausted her edibles for the day, and when they did, they had one or two things to complain about. Either her shop was unsanitary, or the ogi was too lumpy or watery, or the akara had too much or too little salt. Felicia simply laughed off the juju rumour and said aloud to everyone who cared to listen, "Silence is the best answer to a fool. Even better, it's the best answer to an over-bleached elephant like someone we all know." A few women laughed at that and whispered into each other's ears.

Felicia knew her reply would reach its intended ears, for you do not send a gossiper to the marketplace.

Now, Big Mama T had a chance to hit Felicia even harder. She continued her gossip on an issue she had little or no understanding about. "The man thief millions and millions of naira wey government suppose to use and do better railways and trains for we, the Nigerian people. He carry the money chop alone with him family until dem catch am." She clapped her hands as if to exaggerate the arrest. She breathed heavily as she spoke due to her weight. "Thank God say dem catch am before he collapse the whole economy," another woman chipped in. If Felicia didn't know these gossipers, who only seemed out to tarnish her immaculate image of fifteen years in the Egbeda Market, she would have jumped into the discussion to learn more about this thief of a person responsible for the ruin of the entire nation. She would have asked if this man was a government contractor to have had the chance to squander millions of public funds and why the government continued to waste their money on the so-called contractor all these years. She kept her calm and waited to hear, 'Feli-' from their mouths. Then she would knock out their teeth before they'd even finished saying her full name. None of them was brave enough to say who they were referring to though. They simply rolled their eyes and pouted their lips in her direction when she looked away.

The gossip began to gain momentum in the marketplace, and many people stopped patronising Felicia's business as they used to. No one wanted to associate with the wife of the man who had allegedly jeopardised the progress of the entire nation due to his selfishness. Felicia wondered why she had to suffer for an act she'd been oblivious to. If any of the people who had turned their backs on her could think, they would ask themselves why her business had not expanded tremendously after all the embezzlements they claimed her husband had garnered. All these years, she still managed her business in a small aluminium-zinced shed with two long benches where her customers sat, resting their feet on her well-swept cemented floor while she steamed herself sitting on a small stool, frying countless batches of akara balls in a hot pan of oil above layers of blazing firewood. She wondered how that was wealth.

The embarrassment and ridicule she faced daily in her shop, at church and in her neighbourhood finally caused her to consider relocating to the village as her husband had suggested.

"*Atiam* Akpana." She tapped Gregory on his left foot, calling him by the title 'father of Akpana', the name of their first child. In the Nigerian culture, many couples preferred to call their spouses as being the mother or father of a child they shared.

"Atiam Akpana, wake up, please," she called again, shaking him to consciousness.

Gregory awoke with a loud snort.

"We need to talk," she said.

"Wonderful! At 2 a.m.? Talk about what, woman?"

"There are better things to talk about now than sleep," Felicia replied.

"A man cannot rest during the day and at night, too, *A luta continua. Oya* (hurry). Take the mic. I'm all ears," he said, sitting upright and rubbing sleep from his eyes.

"Atiam Akpana, the kids are troubled with unanswered questions, and my business is suffering badly. On the other hand, you have not managed to secure another job yet. I am bothered."

"Okay, is that news? Is that not why I have been asking you to reconsider your stance on moving to the village? Felicia, we cannot continue like this. The financial strain and embarrassment are getting to me even more as the head of this family."

"You should have thought of that before getting into trouble," Felicia muttered, looking at the grey ceiling fan turning above their heads. It emitted a funny, squeaky sound as it turned.

"Wonderful! I don't blame you, Felicia. 'Uneasy lies the head that wears the crown,' so I won't blame you. Do you think it is easy to be a man, expected to provide and keep the wife and kids happy and well-tended year in and year out?"

"We would have managed if you had come plain about your exact salary. I would have understood and made do with what we had."

"Easier said than done," Gregory muttered, focusing his gaze on the blue-painted wall, chipping from a lack of maintenance.

"Look, Felicia," he continued, "I do not have the energy for this kind of conversation at this time of day. Obudu, it is, and that is a full stop, so brace yourself and let bygones be bygones."

Gregory was aloof when it came to displaying his emotions. His wife wanted an apology from him for his bad decisions and the shame they had birthed. She hoped he would thank and encourage her for her financial contributions to the family and assure her of good things to come. Instead, as usual, he acted like the cold and defensive man he was, leaving a teary woman hanging while he turned around to doze off. Without any remorse, he would draw nearer to his wife in the wee hours of the morning and crawl against her skin like a wiggly worm looking for warmth. He would then proceed to reach for the ends of her wrapper and unravel it with haste, not minding the vacuum in the heart of its owner.

****

The children occasionally eavesdropped on their parents' constant bickering about money, travelling and everything else. Their father had become irritable, making the home uncomfortable. They suspected he thought of himself as less of a man for being unable to provide their basic needs, so they excused what they believed was his coping mechanism, which was his aggressive approach to maintaining respect as the head of his home.

One evening, Gregory was approached by his first daughter, Akpana, as he scrolled through countless TV channels. "*Apa* (Daddy)," she said. "The leftover soup from three days ago is finished, sir. There is nothing to eat before bed."

"Wonderful! Nothing for dinner, you say? Am I working, Akpana?"

"No, sir."

"No. Tell me: did you see me with any money in my pockets?" Gregory asked, pulling out his empty trouser pockets to prove he had nothing on him. "Or should I cut off my hand for you people to eat so you all can be filled up?"

"No, sir," Akpana replied.

"All you people know how to do is to eat, play and watch television. The other children winning scholarships and doing big things for their families, do they have two heads?" Gregory asked.

"This year, nobody came first position in school, but in the case of food, you will devour it like hungry lionesses. My friend, go and wait for your mother to return from the shop or drink plenty of water and go to bed." He concluded his speech by curling his legs on the sofa and staring blankly at the giant television screen hung on the wall.

"Yes, sir!" Akpana replied, hastening her steps away from her father.

The other children had been eavesdropping behind their bedroom door. When they heard their father's high-pitched, soprano voice rambling inaudibly, they suspected their stomachs might be required to call it a day.

"What did Apa say?" Beyin, the fourth daughter, asked anxiously as Akpana walked into their small bedroom, silent and not sure how to convey the message.

"Did he give you money to buy *indomie* noodles or bread, at least?" Atimanu, the third daughter, asked.

"Apa said we should wait for *Ama* (Mum) to come back from the shop," Akpana muttered soberly.

"And what does that mean, exactly? We don't even know when Ama is coming back from the shop," Udanshi, the second daughter, queried.

"Oh, my tummy!" little Amokeye screamed, throwing herself dramatically to their marble-tiled floor. She held her tummy and kicked her feet in the air as she cried and screamed her lungs out as most 'babies of the house' would.

"Don't let Apa hear you, o," Adeshi, the fifth daughter, advised her little sister just before their father could address the inconsolable child.

"Who is that whining like a dog there? If I meet you with my belt, you will smell pepper before going to bed."

"Who will smell pepper this night?" Felicia asked, walking into the living room, where the door had been left open for the evening fresh air to breeze in. She had just returned from her daily sales when she'd heard her husband's shrill voice thundering from the staircase that led to their flat on the second floor of the building.

"Ama, Ama—I am hungry," little Amokeye said, running into her mother's arms.

"Will you eat akara and ogi?" her mother asked with a hopeless stare.

"Akara and ogi, again?" Amokeye questioned.

"If you don't want to eat it, then go and sleep," her father retorted.

"Gregory, enough of these rants. *Haba*! What is this vexation all these days for?"

"Wonderful! Felicia, you dare insult me before these children by calling my speech rants?" Gregory asked, uncurling his legs from the grey sofa to face his wife squarely. The sofa chair was his favourite place to sit and relax. Even visitors knew the grey sofa belonged to the man of the house and steered clear of sitting there. It was on that chair that Felicia and the kids served his meals while he watched the LG television mounted above the DSTV decoder table. Sometimes, he dozed off on it while watching his favourite TVC news at 10 p.m. Unfortunately, the once happy chair was now a place of gloom and sorrow, where its owner sat whimpering over his loss and the uncertainty of the future.

"I don't blame you," Gregory continued, staring his petite wife in the eyes, slightly beneath his chest. He was a huge man, about six feet tall, quite robust, with a masculine carriage. He didn't speak very often, and many people claimed Felicia was lucky to be married to such a reserved gentleman, but keeping silent was best for everyone who came across Gregory. The gross mismatch between his masculine frame and his ear-piercing falsetto caused people to wonder if the voice came from his mouth or a figure behind him. His unique voice didn't make his new status as a stay-at-home husband easy for his ego, but he was determined to reclaim his head of the house mantle by any means necessary.

So, he stood upright on their marble-tiled floor, allowing his macho frame to reiterate his speech as he continued to quarrel with his wife. "Since you became the man of this house, returning home to me, your wife, things have not remained the same. And now you insult me in front of my children. My eyes have finally seen my ears."

"What kind of accusation is that, eh, Gregory? One day, one trouble. Is this what I get for all the trouble I go through for our family? God knows I am tired of you and your everyday problems. I am tired!" Felicia exclaimed.

"Wonderful! Then leave—what are you waiting for, Felicia? Is that not what you women do when your husbands are financially handicapped? After all these years of providing, a short season of lack has become unbearable. Just make sure you leave my daughters behind for me. That's all!"

Felicia swallowed a mouth of spittle down her patched throat, her palm clutching tightly to her waist purse. Last week, the Catholic Women's Organisation president led a segment on Mother's Day, teaching the wives and mothers to be submissive to their husbands regardless of their attitude towards them. If any of the women could not control their lousy mouths when their husbands scolded and corrected them, they must fill their mouths with water to prevent them from talking back or block their ears with cotton wool. Felicia had accumulated a good quantity of saliva in her mouth in place of water and swallowed it. She'd waited for Gregory to return to his seat before hurrying into their narrow kitchen, exhausted from her daily sales and arguing with her husband. If she had left earlier, it would have been a case of Felicia-walking-out-on-her-husband. Her older daughters Akpana, Udanshi and Atimanu, assisted with her ogi coolers and the large trays she placed her akara on while on display.

Meanwhile, the younger ones, Beyin and Adeshi, tagged along with little Amokeye, who was dragging her feet with her head tilted backwards.

Gregory's attempt to get words out of Felicia would not work, she told herself. Three days prior, she had lovingly asked him why he had not at least supervised the younger kids in doing the dishes so she could have a neat space to fix the family dinner after returning from the market. Her husband made a similar allegation: "If I had a job like my mates out there, would you consider me a kitchen supervisor?"

"You people will eat akara and ogi tonight, okay? I will try my best to buy *agege* bread tomorrow morning with tea, okay?" Her girls nodded reluctantly, shedding tears as they scraped the leftover ogi from their mother's food cooler. Their home had lost its flavour since the unfortunate incident that had befallen their father. There was no laughter, no TV time, no love and worst of all, barely any food except the leftovers from their mother's business that she couldn't sell.

The Carnival

It was a busy week in Gowon Estate, Egbeda, Lagos. Both the young and the old prepared for the annual end-of-the-year carnival. On that day, many business owners laughed all the way to the bank, and Felicia wanted a piece of that joy for her family as well. She had registered her interest in selling that year, paying a fee to the carnival committee and securing a few stands where fresh money was to be made. Being a smart businesswoman, Felicia journeyed all the way to the Oshodi Market to buy both soft and alcoholic drinks as well as wholesale edibles. She wrapped her bargains in big sacks, and she and Akpana placed a sack on their heads and hopped from bus to bus en route to their home in Egbeda, where they carefully stacked their buys in the backyard of their two-bedroom, rented flat in Gowon Estate.

Gowon Estate was a chill, bubbly place to live in, with blocks of flats that had been built by the former Nigerian

Military Head of State General Yakubu Gowon in 1977 to house participants during the World Festival of Art and Culture (FESTAC). After the events, the estate buildings were distributed to government agencies and parastatals, such as the Nigerian Navy, Army, Police forces, Nigerian Airways, Customs, State Security services (SSS), Foreign Affairs, and Banks, amongst others. The workers of these agencies and parastatals lived in the tall buildings for a discounted price from their take-home salaries. In turn, some workers had, rented out their government homes to ordinary citizens as an extra source of income. Mr Gregory had rented his two-bedroom flat from a Naval officer who had no need for the property due to his regular postings across the country for work. The estate was a safe place to live. Thieves and armed robbers thought twice before visiting the estate, surrounded majorly by armed forces.

Estate dwellers pulled resources together to organise yearly events, such as the annual carnival, which kept young minds busy and sprung hidden talents, some of which were later discovered to have better stayed hidden. Young boys and girls mounted the stage to show the stuff they were made of, singing, dancing, rapping or cracking jokes to either boos or applause.

The event also generated a lot of money for businesses as it ushered in loads of visitors from within and outside Lagos State, who came to see celebrity guests like Jaywon, who visited to sing the famous end of the year/new year hit single, 'This Year'. The crowd always sang their hearts out to the blissful lyrics that talked about being prosperous in the new year.

That year, Felicia took a loan from the Lift Above Poverty Organisation (LAPO) to help her buy alcoholic and soft drinks, like La Casera, Coke, Fanta, the famous Viju and Bobo milk in apple and orange flavours from Oshodi Market. If her conscience let her, she would also sell cigarettes to make more money, as many attending the carnival were heavy smokers, but she dilly-dallied about the decision and waited until the last minute.

As usual, the price of these items doubled and tripled during the event, and to make a lot of money, all Felicia needed to do was set up stalls at strategic places and make sure her drinks were ice cold. To that end, she'd wrapped water in ice bags and placed them in her deep freezer many days before.

Felicia was a dynamic woman who seized every opportunity to make money, and considering her family's woes, Gregory had to join in that year's sales. Together, they would create an even bigger sale to earn just enough money to start life afresh when they finally left for Obudu in the new year.

The day of the carnival was eventful. Akpana carefully chiselled out large blocks of ice that had stuck to each other in the deep freezer and placed many of them in a round bath basin Nigerians like to call a *baff*. She moulded an old piece of wrapper spirally and placed it on her head to support her baff, which was filled with ice blocks, and walked past the crowd of people having fun at the carnival. Some sang and danced to the music coming from the gigantic speakers mounted on the high stage, while others bought and sold carnival essentials by the roadside. Many young people made out and giggled softly in dark corners. Akpana saw one of her former classmates sitting on a boy's lap, saying something inaudible. "God forbid!" Akpana muttered, walking briskly by to avoid being seen.

Felicia was already setting up one of her stalls with a wide table and various drinks, chocolates, and cigarettes on display. She had two other stalls strategically set where customers would likely pass by.

Beyin and her dad camped out in one stall, and Atimanu and her oldest sister, Akpana, had one to themselves. Adeshi and little Amokeye stayed home because the event was inappropriate for their age, while Udanshi, aka UD, was assigned to help their mother in her stall.

"Are you the only one bringing the ice blocks? Where is UD?" Felicia asked, lifting the bath basin from Akpana's head.

"I thought she was with you. She told me she was coming to help you set up your stall," Akpana replied.

"Ah, ah…but I asked her to come and assist you to make your trip quicker…or is she with your dad?"

"No, Ma. I passed by his stall, and she wasn't there."

"Could she have gone to keep Atimanu company before your arrival?"

"She isn't there, either. I dropped some ice blocks there before coming here."

"Ah, ah…don't tell me UD has started *kukere-waka o* (rugged movement), with all these wolverines around here. Where is my daughter? Where is Udanshi?" Felicia screamed with frightful eyes, looking for answers from a crowd of unknown faces partying hard on the football field where the carnival was being held.

"I'm here, Ma," a squeaky voice making its way from the corner shop replied hastily.

"And where are you coming from?"

"I…I…I was just gist…gisting with my friends, Ma," UD stammered nervously as her left eye twitched. Whenever she was in a compromising situation, her left eye gave her away, twitching uncontrollably.

"Friends, *abi* (right)?" Felicia asked, looking straight into the twitching eye to let her know her game was up. "You must think I was born yesterday, but no problem. Let me face my business first. We shall continue this conversation when we get home. For now, sit your butt on that chair where I can monitor you closely."

"Yes, Ma," UD said, adjusting her short, stretchy skirt to reach her knees.

Her mother shook her head and sighed. "Have you shattered the ice?" she turned back and asked Akpana, determined not to let some silly child ruin her business activities.

"I have done some, Ma," Akpana replied faithfully.

The shattered ice was placed in a hundred-litre cooler. Soft drinks were placed on top of the ice to keep them cool. Another block of ice was placed on top of the drinks. The worst thing that could happen to any seller on carnival day was to have warm drinks that nobody would buy. UD gave a nasty glance to her big sister Akpana, who immediately got the message. She was expected to cover her sister's misdeeds as usual but not that night. Akpana ignored the glance and picked up her bath basin to get another set of ice blocks.

The carnival went well. Felicia had many boys troop into her stall to patronise her drinks because of the beauty standing by her. UD was a beauty to behold, a dark-skinned damsel with two pothole-like dimples on the sides of her chubby face. "Help me to buy, nau," she called to admirers. One glance towards the nightingale caused buyers to leave the stalls they'd initially intended to patronise to pay for UD's drinks.

"Malta Guinness, Star and Heineken, na three hundred and fifty naira a can," she said in pidgin English, pointing to the drinks. "Viju and Bobo Milk na two hundred and fifty naira per bottle." Felicia pretended not to notice that her daughter had suddenly hiked the price further by adding an extra fifty naira to all the drinks. It was a carnival, and all was fair on a day like today.

"Ama," UD called her mother when the noise from the loudspeakers had quietened a bit.

"Anything?" Felicia responded while stacking cigarettes on her display table.

"I don't want the village life. I want to stay here with my friends, continue my dance classes and live my life to the fullest."

"Ehen? So you can't live life to the fullest in your hometown?" Felicia asked, slightly irritated.

"Viju milk na two hundred and fifty naira, dear," UD told a prospective buyer.

"But others are selling for two hundred naira," the buyer responded.

"Oya, bring two hundred naira just because I like you." UD smiled, handed out a bottle of chilled Viju milk from the cooler and replaced it with a warmer one to chill.

"Ama, but you know life is tougher over there," UD said, continuing the conversation. "The farm life, the bloodsucking insects that feast on the flesh with a fork and knife, and I can't seem to wrap my head around the fact that I shall be interacting with stack illiterates, people who cannot manage a simple English construction. I fear my IQ will be drastically reduced, not to mention the dangers of living amongst witches and wizards. Ama, don't tell me my life is over before it starts. Please, I don't want to die now o—"

"Shut up your dirty mouth, drama queen! Are you suffering from diarrhoea of the mouth, or is your brain overheating?" Felicia interrupted angrily, raising her head to her daughter, who had grown so tall, just like her father. If it were not for some grey hairs here and there, children would mistake height for age. UD quickly looked away briefly as a sign of respect; looking an elder in the eye was a sign of disrespect in many cultures in Nigeria.

"Ah Ah…Ama, what have I said to warrant those bad words?"

"You are not serious. Were your father and I not born in the village before coming to the city for greener pastures? If anybody had eaten our flesh for fetish reasons, would we be alive today to birth you and your sisters? And what IQ do you speak of, by the way? Same IQ that earned you nine Ds and three Es in your last Junior WAEC, where they managed to push you to SS1 in the spirit of 'let my people go?'"

UD felt embarrassed. She passed a pack of cigarettes to a buyer quietly and collected a five hundred naira note from him.

"Keep the change," the lanky man said, turning his back to light a cigarette stick.

"Thanks, sir," UD replied with a fake smile from the ill mood her mother had put her in. This would be the sixtieth time, if not more, that her mother was rubbing her below-average performance in her face to put her in a corner. However, she shook off the insults. After all, she'd passed from JSS3 to SS1, unlike others who had to reseat the Junior WAEC examination.

"But Ama," UD said, having regained some confidence, "that's not the issue. All I am saying is that we can still manage here in Lagos. Apa can find something else to do here with time. I'm just concerned about my mental health living in the village."

"My, me, I, everything about Udanshi is always about herself, not others. At your father's age, you expect him to carry concrete on his head on building sites, or you expect him to sell water as the *mai ruwa's* do so we can survive in Lagos, right? In fact, I'm happy that we are moving to the village so you can learn a thing or two from the village life. You should see how your younger cousin Iye pounds yam for her mother: very smooth, with no lumps, at her age. Linda, born the same year as you, farms like a man, digging, planting and harvesting. She carries the farm produce on her head and walks five miles back home. With those lazy bones of yours, would you dare to try such a thing? What do they call the other one? ehm —"

"Well done, my sister," a voice interrupted the conversation. It was Sister Alice from the Church of Harvest of Bliss and Plenty, where Felicia secretly attended miracle services despite being Catholic. There, she sought the face of the Lord from a group of prophesiers who told her what her enemies had planned for her family. Sister Alice was one of the prophetesses, and on that night, she was dressed in a baggy pleated skirt, a chiffon blouse with shoulder pads, and a turban scarf wrapped around her forehead. That unique dress sense was to announce her as a born-again Christian to everyone who cared to know. It separated her from the world and all its pleasures, which were considered vain. Some of the Harvesters, as they liked to call themselves, embraced that extreme dress sense — hair extensions and trousers for ladies were strictly prohibited. Women were to appear holy and modest, with a knee-length skirt or dress, and no make-ups.

Felicia only let her daughters wear trousers in the house. Once they were out of the house, they either concealed their trousers with a wrapper around their waists or changed to knee-length dresses or skirts. Felicia also occasionally allowed them to use attachments for braiding their hair, but she never let them use weaves, as this was considered more extreme and unholy compared to attachments like wool, thread, and braid extensions, which looked minimal and decent.

People like Sister Alice ensured these standards were maintained within the church group. If she wasn't coaching members about their waywardness by word of mouth, she did it with her eyes while clapping her hands with an intense velocity at prayer meetings. If you came to a meeting without a proper head covering, her eyes scanned your head for minutes, and she offered you a use and return handkerchief.

If your dress was too short, she signalled for you to sit in the back so you would not tempt the brothers who lifted their holy hands in worship. If you wore a pair of trousers to a meeting in the name of coming directly from your workplace, you were ushered to sit outside the church and listen through the vast loudspeakers strategically mounted outside the church so the unbelievers and non-churchgoers could hear.

The same loudspeakers were mounted on the carnival stage. The only difference was that the former echoed songs glorifying God and His heavenly throne, while the latter amplified songs glorifying worldly pleasures.

However deafening the speakers were, Felicia could never miss Sister Alice's croaky voice, not even while asleep. It was the same croaky voice that screamed while preaching in prayer meetings: "Repent! Repent for the kingdom of God is at hand!"

Sometimes, people claimed her voice stuck in their ears, ringing for weeks with messages of salvation.

"Ah, Sister Alice, good to see you here." Felicia returned her salutation. "You want to buy something?"

"Buy something? What could a child of God like me buy from a place like this? I am just here for some evening fresh air, but I doubt I'll get any with all this deadly smoke flying about."

Felicia kept her mouth shut; her lips pressed tightly together. Sister Alice was obviously going somewhere with her conversation, especially with her gaze on the pyramid of stacked up cigarettes.

"I can see you added cigarettes to your sales this year," Sister Alice blurted.

"Yes, you see clearly," Felicia replied.

Sister Alice took a deep breath, looking quite concerned. "I am just worried about your salvation, my dear sister. Last year, you moved from selling soft drinks to alcohol, and this year, you have graduated to selling cigarettes. I wonder what you will sell next year. Remember, the Bible says, in the book of—"

"In the book of what? Sister Alice in Wonderland! Eh? You know what? I am considering selling *igbo* (weed), next year—"

"Igbo!" Sister Alice exclaimed, her mouth and eyes wide open in astonishment.

"Yes, you heard me right, Alice, Igbo. After all, my cherished customers have been asking. So, take your hypocrisy elsewhere, and let God be my judge. Have a good night and enjoy your fresh air," Felicia replied with bloodshot eyes, moving swiftly from her position and backing her guest to arrange nothing in particular on the busy table.

Sister Alice disappeared into the crowd. The scenario between her and Felicia would make an excellent example in the coming weeks' prayer meetings about backsliding soldiers, the love of money, and storing up treasures on earth.

"Imagine this hypocrite talking rubbish to me like she's holier than thou. Who does she think she is, eh? By the way, what is she, a single born-again prayer leader, doing in the carnival...or did she miss her way to a Church crusade? Nonsense individual!" Felicia said.

Amused by the cacophony of events, UD had had a good belly laugh behind the scenes, holding her tummy to the floor to avoid her mother's look. Sister Alice had caused her mother to speak a big grammar: "Nonsense Individual!" Her sisters must hear about it, and together, they would have a good laugh and begin to call each other "Nonsense individuals!"

Felicia didn't know who annoyed her more: her daughter—who referred to her people as witches and stacked illiterates for not speaking proper English—or Sister Alice, who was like a virgin in a maternity ward. Sister Alice was just being a hypocrite. As for her daughter? She didn't blame her much. UD and her siblings had been brought up in Lagos, and they had heard many ill stories about the villagers from lousy storytellers there. Each time they scolded the children about being wasteful, they reminded them of the starving children in the village who didn't have the same luxury of a variety of meals or the fancy clothes they wore. They talked about the villagers' lack of basic amenities, like motorable roads, good hospitals, electricity and drinkable water, and how their poor English grammar presented them as an inferior group of people who needed to be helped and pitied. They learnt about the villagers' jealousy because they had few resources to go around and how they envied those who flourished. That envy had allegedly led to witchcraft, with some villagers being accused of going diabolical and causing harm to their fellow beings for daring to rise above them.

However, the city brought ups were never told how much the villagers had prospered against all odds. Though they had no sophisticated farm equipment, they worked hard with the basics, producing good harvests each year. As they had little money for transportation, they walked many miles with their *legediz benz*(legs), a natural exercise that burnt calories and kept them healthy. Their lack of refrigerators caused them to eat freshly made foods daily. Though they had no fancy swimming pools to show affluence like the city kids, they did have a cool stream where freshwater flowed daily. From there, they did their laundry and took cool baths in the scorching sun, enjoying the lovely weather with minimal worries, all surrounded by nature to the tune of tweeting birds. They breathed fresher air because of the low emissions from fossil fuels in the rural area and the beautiful trees surrounding their homes, from which they plucked fresh fruit at no cost and lived healthily. Their absence of televisions may have deprived them of motion pictures, but it improved their human interaction. As a substitute for *Tom and Jerry, Johnny Bravo, Pinky and the Brain* and the like, they had lovely storytellers who told thoughtfully beautiful stories full of moral lessons as they sat in a large circle, singing along in the fantastic evening just beneath the stars and the moon until they fell asleep on the mat, enjoying the refreshing breeze of the night till morning.

The village elites read newspapers and listened to AM/FM stations broadcasting from small dry cell radio transmitters, and they were well-informed about the news around the world.

The fact that they did not speak fluent English should never have been a yardstick for measuring their intelligence. They were professionals in their mother tongue and spoke all the *Bette*-African proverbs, something the city people could never boast of.

They barely fell ill because of how active their bodies were and how much immunity they had built up over the years, but when they did fall ill, they had professional herbalists who prescribed natural remedies that worked well for the people. So, even though they lacked good hospitals, many of them lived longer than those in the city.

Unfortunately, when the city people lost their lives or fell ill for whatever reason, they blamed it on the very old and healthy villagers, accusing them of witchcraft and bloodsucking, a theory that brought about the popular Nigerian description of bad luck as 'the work of my village people'.

Many villagers were aware of this perception of them, that they were inferior, envious, pained and needed to be pitied.

These misconceptions and more made Felicia ignore her daughter. She believed her daughter would have a different mindset when she met with the villagers.

Farewell

Felicia had amassed significant money from the Carnival sale, enough to repay LAPO and support her family's journey to Obudu in the new year. Their impending departure saddened the Bebuagbong Village community in Lagos. They had formed an excellent bond over the years, fighting and making up, hosting meetings, and eating from each other's pots. Now, it was time to bid the Gregory family goodbye in their customary manner. Some financial contributions were made to support them, and some of Felicia's friends volunteered to sleep over to help cook for the farewell party.

Everyone had shown up in style for the party. The women came nicely dressed in their red *gele* (scarf) and two-piece bird feather design Hollandis wrapper with a yellow lace top sewn in different styles according to the taste of its owner. The men coordinated with the women, dressed in sewn bird feather design trousers and kaftan tops that had little or no embellishments but were just plain and simple. That was the attire chosen for casual outings, and everyone came looking their best. The women compared stylish blouses and asked for each other's tailor contact. The younger wives, known for their trendsetting, added unique embellishments to their sewn blouses and skirts to the amusement of the older wives. These days, younger women prefer to sew skirts or gowns in place of the standard two-piece wrappers worn by mothers back in the day.

"*Uwhangie* (young wife), you are glowing, o. It shows that our brother is looking after you very well," one chubby woman said, her mouth full of Nigerian jollof rice. She was referring to the latest wife, who had just been married into the family. "Soon enough, that blouse will be too tight from your growing tummy." Laughter and joyful voices filled the air.

The young wife joined the other voices in screaming a massive "Amen!"

"When that time comes," the chubby woman continued, "you won't even remember to wear lipstick, so enjoy your time with Jonah before the babies start trooping in."

Voices from the corners laughed and chattered about what life before kids was like.

The young wife smiled gently. She knew the pressure to start making babies was beginning to build up. If only these old schools knew she and Jonah had agreed to enjoy their marriage for three years before bringing any humans into the world, but that was a piece of crippling news that would knock them off their seats.

Mrs Felicia and her helpers cooked a large pot of smoky jollof rice with fried turkey. Many African men preferred to eat fufu and soup at events to show some manliness. So, the women prepared some fufu, a West African starchy side dish made from cassava. The soup for the fufu was the famous *uhwe kanakel* (groundnut soup), with large chunks of dried fish and beef for garnishing. The pleasant aroma of pepper soup with assorted cow parts filled the air. Many African snacks, like puff-puffs, meat pies, and chin-chins, were present to keep the younger ones' mouths busy while they played catch-up with their peers.

On the other hand, Gregory had bought crates of beer, soft drinks, and bottles of wine to make their send-off party from Lagos one-in-town, regardless of his financial abilities. A day like that was not one to wash dirty linens in public. Well-wishers didn't come empty-handed, either — some brought kola nuts, bottles of wine, and new household items to bid their hosts farewell.

Customarily, the people's culture is never hidden. A drummer graced the occasion with traditional rhythmic beats that brought joyful and nostalgic reactions as the people recollected memories of life in Obudu before they all sought greener pastures in the multicultural Lagos City.

The drums transitioned the people into a different realm as the sound of women ululating filled the air. Hands swung about, and heads nodded with feet moving one step at a time as their bent waists swung in a calculated fashion around the drummers.

To heighten the artistic tapestry of the dance moves and the passion they ignited, the drummers began playing another familiar beat. The contagious sound brought about a euphoric reaction as the people screamed, "*hey!*" to show their preparedness for some bursting dance moves.

Gregory's lawyer and best friend, Barrister Donatus, was tipsy after drinking a few cups of palm wine. It was no legal day to be uptight and professional, so he'd let himself loose, staggering to the beats of the drums and moving his feet here and there as if he were kicking an invisible football in the air. Then, he bent over and wiggled his hips like the ladies. There was an outburst of cheer from the crowd, with some guests dropping from their seats to the gravelled floor in uncontrollable laughter.

"The law!" they shouted randomly, hailing the tipsy barrister.

"My dad stays clowning to my embarrassment," Odette, Barrister Donatus' daughter, told her friend, Akpana.

"You should thank your stars for your dad's jovial nature. At least he knows when to party and when to be serious, unlike mine, a perpetual no-nonsense fellow," Akpana replied, half laughing.

The two girls chuckled at the words 'no-nonsense fellow.'

"I wonder how they have managed to stay best of friends after all these years," Akpana said.

"Unlike poles attract, don't they?" Odette teased.

The girls laughed again.

Odette quickly changed the conversation as she could no longer stand her father in his merry state. "So, now that you have been admitted to the University of Port Harcourt to study computer science, what are your plans for accommodation? I hope you do not intend to stay off campus and miss out on all the fun in the student's hostel as my big sister Ngozi did?"

"Well, that is if I don't defer my admission," Akpana said, looking away.

"What do you mean by that?" Odette questioned, feeling concerned.

"Can't you see that my parents are struggling financially? I mean, they hate to admit it, but the financial struggle in our house is as clear as day."

"Hmmm…I hear you, Akpana, but the Uncle Gregory that I know would go to any length to make sure you do not miss school or defer your admission, even if it meant borrowing to pay your school fees. I trust him about that," Odette said.

"Well, let's see," Akpana replied.

"So, back to my question: will you be on or off campus?"

Akpana chuckled lightly. "If you know how long I have waited for this opportunity to see the world and mingle joyfully with other cultures, you wouldn't even ask about that. I mean, all my life, my parents have shielded me like the world possesses some kind of virus. Although I'm their first daughter, they seem not to know when to let me test my wings. You know what I mean."

"I feel you," Odette said.

"This is my chance, Odette, and I won't trade it for any safety net my parents plan for me." As Akpana spoke, tears gathered in her eyes. Odette quickly reached for her hands and held them tightly in solidarity.

"So, does that mean you are staying on campus?"

"Of course!" Akpana screamed, her teary eyes wide open.

"That's the spirit, girl! Just do you, and you'll be fine, just remember—"

"Odette!" a voice called from a distance. It was Madam Chinyere, Odette's mother.

"Ma!"

"Come and prepare. We need to set off before dark."

"Yes, Ma."

"Just remember who you are," Odette continued. "Whatever exposure you seek, just be careful. We don't want a police case o."

"Oh no! Police, *keh*?" Akpana asked while laughing, marvelling at her friend's audacity towards life. Akpana had never thought about having a police case, so she was surprised it had ever crossed Odette's mind. When Odette said things like that, she spoke with a lot of confidence and exposure. Akpana admired her and wished her dad had let her go to a boarding secondary school far away from Lagos as Barrister Donatus had done with his kids. All of his kids could speak at least two to three Nigerian languages. Donatus Junior, Odette's older brother, could speak Igbo, his eastern local dialect, Yoruba, the language of Lagos, where he was born and Efik, the language of the Calabar people, where he had attended boarding school in St. Patricks College (SPC). Odette could also speak Yoruba, Igbo and Hausa, the language of the Northerners, where she and her big sister Ngozi had been schooled at Federal Government Girls' College Keana. Conversely, Gregory believed it was best to let the kids go to school from home so he could keep a good eye on them, an action that came with its own problems, namely a lack of exposure.

"But I will miss you, *sha*. Who else would give me loads of gist and listen to my banter as you do?" Odette asked.

"Come off it, girl. You speak like I'm going to a different planet or something. Besides, we can talk on video calls, and I can visit Lagos occasionally."

"Do they even have any network connections over there?"

"Of course, Odette! Obudu is not a forest. Educate yourself, young lady."

The friends laughed hysterically at their naivety of rural life.

"Odette!" Madam Chinyere called her daughter again. "Are you still standing there gisting and laughing? Don't let me land my slippers at the back of your oblong head. I said we must leave before dark. I don't want Lagos a*gberos* (hoodlums) to take advantage of the time of the day to increase the transportation fee, so hurry up."

"Yes, Ma!" Odette replied to her mum.

"Okay, Akpana. I must go now. Just bring it in. One last hug until we meet again."

"Please keep in touch, Odette."

"I promise I will." Odette and Akpana hugged each other, shedding and wiping tears as they slowly parted from each other's embrace.

Goodbye Lagos

Travelling by land had proven to be a stressful experience for Akpana. She had once represented her secondary school in various Scrabble competitions within Lagos. One time, she was required to travel hundreds of kilometres to where the competition occurred in a rural school somewhere in Akwa-Ibom State in the southern part of Nigeria.

At the beginning of the trip, she decided to buy some ripe bananas and groundnuts from the women at the motor park in Iyana-Ipaja.

"Buy yah banana! sweet-sweet banana!" one trader called out loud. She was carrying a tray of ripe bananas of various sizes and small wrapped bags of groundnuts, skilfully arranged on her large tray that sat comfortably on an old piece of wrapper spiralled on her head. The bananas looked very juicy. They poked Akpana's eyes as the trader came closer, arousing her appetite and that of prospective buyers. After fighting the thought of purchasing some, she finally gave in to her long throat and bought a bunch of small ripe bananas and two wraps of groundnut from the pocket money her father had given her for the journey. The combination of banana and groundnut was the greatest ever; the creamy, mashed bananas with the salty, crunchy groundnuts did a heavenly, salivary tango as they were crushed in the mouth and slid down the oesophagus. Whoever the inventor of this all-time favourite combination was, they would make it to heaven for discovering the mix, she told herself while savouring the nutty vanilla flavour of each mouthful. By the time the bus had conveyed them over one hundred kilometres to Ogun State, almost everyone around Akpana had been baptised by her vomit. The lady directly in front of her had cussed out after her wig was drenched with the slimy puke. The man next to the lady, who had also had a generous share of the nutty vanilla-spiced mixture, gagged, sighed and hissed until his mouth went dry.

"Why must you eat bananas and groundnuts at the start of your journey, young girl? Don't you know that certain foods could trigger tummy upset due to the potholes on the road, the smell of petrol or even the fumes from exhaust pipes?" The furious bus driver asked, cleaning some slime that had reached his leather seat. He was forced to park his eighteen-seater bus by the roadside, surrounded by a thick green forest.

"Now, you must hurry and clean up. This place is not safe for stopping," he said.

"She is sorry, everyone. She is just a child, and it's her first time travelling. Apologies, please," Akpana's school guardian said on behalf of the sickly culprit, who was standing in the corner of the bus like a frozen chicken with a chapped voice.

The passengers began cleaning up the spew, some from their shoes, others from their faces. A few had a quick change of clothing by the side of the bus facing the green forest. The lady with the wig had no choice but to remove her artificial hair, revealing nasty cornrows that had probably been done months ago.

"Ah ah, *sisi sisi Eko* (young lady of Lagos), is this your real face?" one lanky transporter asked the wig lady as he wiped his trousers with a wet handkerchief. "So, with all that *shakara* (show off) you were doing when I asked for your phone number, this is actually your real face?"

The travellers laughed out loud as the defenceless lady ignored him with a frowny face. She had no choice; it was either the nasty cornrow reveal and a mockery or wearing a filthy, slimy hair wig for the rest of their journey.

Poor Akpana — how was she to know she would be one of those people who should never taste any food or water before a long-distance trip due to motion sickness? She had always been protected, like an egg, and had never crossed a long distance to explore what might or might not be a problem with her body system.

Akpana remembered that experience and was determined not to let her history with motion sickness repeat itself. On the morning of her family's move from Lagos to Obudu, she refused to eat or drink anything when she was woken up to prepare to catch the bus leaving for Ojuelegba Motor Park. Her parents had sent a good chunk of their property ahead to Obudu many days ago. Friends and well-wishers had assisted the family with moving their heavy sofas and beds into a truck with an inscription on it: Iya Suleiman and Sons Ventures. Now, it was time to transport the family.

Udanshi, Beyin, Atimanu, Adeshi and little Amokeye scrambled into their small bathroom and toilet cubicle at 3 a.m., when they heard their mother's scream: "Wake up!" The way they jumped up from their spread-out mats and scrambled into their bathroom reminded their mother of the biblical descriptions of the enemies of God's children that said: "They shall come against you in one direction but shall flee in seven," and another that stated, "Their path shall be dark and slippery as the angel of the Lord pursues them." Like "the wicked running when no one pursued," they bumped their heads into each other, tripping and rolling over as they tried to navigate the space between them and the bathroom. UD and Beyin stood facing opposite directions, brushing their teeth over the bathroom sink, while Atimanu and Adeshi entered the bath to take a simultaneous quick shower to speed up the activities. Little Amokeye was doing a number two with sleepy eyes and nearly fell into the toilet at different times.

As the eldest daughter, an already awoken Akpana had been relegated to make breakfast for her younger siblings: six packs of 'Hungry Man' noodles and four scrambled eggs. Before starting their journey, they would eat at the Cross Lines Motor Park in Ojuelegba.

"Did you put my slippers in my handbag, Beyin?" asked Felicia.

"Yes, Ma."

"What about paracetamol, nylon bags and cloves for the vomiting people?"

"Where should I put those ones, Ma?"

"Put them on my head," Felicia said sarcastically.

"If you people do not leave this house in the next ten minutes, you will all meet me in Obudu," Gregory threatened. The children hurried out of the house. Their father had a good mind of leaving them behind if they wasted his time further. Goose bumps popped out of Akpana's skin as she made her way out of their now-old home that felt so cold and lifeless. No picture frames hung on the walls. Gone were the massive sofas that had taken up the tiny space in the living room, leaving passers-by with less than a metre of space to squabble between the sofas and the humongous centre table to the other parts of the house. The house had been stripped of its splendour, with no curtains to shield them from the prying eyes of curious neighbours in surrounding blocks. For once, their home of many years appeared bare and in desperate need of a covering.

Akpana took a last look around the estate from the second floor, where their flat was situated. Her heart beat faster than usual as she twirled her braids around her fingers anxiously. A new life awaited her family; she hoped it would be as beautiful as the admirable sight of the colourful blocks of flats adding vibrance to the neighbourhood's aesthetics, especially in the dark. The Nigeria Airways blocks, for example, were painted to represent the colours of the Nigerian flag. They were immaculate white with a green inscription in the middle of the three-story building, stating its address. The Navy blocks were painted maroon-red and green. The Union Bank blocks were painted turquoise blue and creamy yellow, the blocks always looked immaculate and peaceful. Most of the occupants were bankers, and that reflected heavily in the aesthetic of their buildings. Their well-cemented landing and shiny security lights made one think of a villa when staring at their quarters at night. While the police blocks came off as dark grey.

Each building communicated its story through its looks.

Whilst admiring the chaotic beauty exuding around her, Akpana smiled softly, relating the sight to life's imperfections. She took a deep breath, inhaling as much of the estate air as her lungs could carry, as if to engrave the scent perpetually in her mind. Some drops of tears trickled down her cheeks, making their way in between the slabs that protected residents from falling off the high building. Akpana watched to see how far the drops would travel before vanishing into the darkness beneath. Adeshi and little Amokeye enjoyed throwing broken sticks down the same hole and watching to see whose stick travelled faster.

Soon the sound of a key lock shook Akpana to reality. Her father had just locked the door upon confirming that all the children and their belongings had made their way out.

Gregory and Felicia carried a large *Ghana Must Go* bag, with Felicia pulling from one side and her husband from the other. Their unbalanced heights made the bag swing in an odd manner, with one side way higher than the other. The girls followed along, each with sizable bags according to their ability. As they moved past one building to the other trying to catch the bus leaving at 4 a.m. from the Egbeda bus stop to the Ojuelegba Motor Park, they looked back at the blocks of the estate, feeling homesick already. The moon seemed to have been hiding its shine from the family, perhaps being gloomy itself, unable to watch them leave their family home of eighteen years. Akpana noticed a few cracks, revealing some heavy iron bars on the side of the police block just beside their quarters. Last year, it was reported that a slab serving as a safety barricade had fallen off the first floor of one of the blocks a mile away. Luckily, nobody was hurt, but it was a significant hazard that meant that the durable Gowon Estate blocks might be losing their strength with age.

"So, this is it," Atimanu thought out loud. "I will miss you, my beloved home." The seemingly strongest of the children cried her eyes out, much to the shock of her siblings. All of them had shed their farewell tears in the days and nights before, while Atimanu had mocked their show of emotion. Now, it was her turn. She proved to be human, too.

****

"Come and enter our bus, sir. We will do you fine, you will see. Our drivers get plenty of experience. No bad driving, you will see," a voice screamed in the crowd of young men and boys.

"Na our bus cheap pass all of them. Try Cross Country Motors and thank me later, sir," a young lad said, pulling Gregory by the arm at the Ojuelegba under-bridge area. The men hustled and canvassed passengers for different transport companies for a commission. They pulled prospective customers by their garments until many gave in and patronised the hustlers' choice of transport company.

Unfortunately, thieves often hid amongst the genuine hustlers, causing havoc. They pretended to convince innocent travellers to come over while snatching their loosely held travelling bags and running out of sight.

Gregory was aware of this dirty trick, so he lectured his girls on how to hold their bags tightly under their armpits.

An elderly *baba,* slightly bent over with brownish tobacco-stained teeth, tapped Gregory on his shoulder. "Try God Is Good Motors, sir. Full air conditioner from Lagos to the south, no offing. Try it, sir; you and your family will love it," he said.

"Wonderful, sir! But I have already booked Cross Lines Motors many days ago. Maybe next time," Gregory replied tactfully. The sides of his mouth widened with a smile, but his eyes did not corroborate the gesture on his lips. As quick as lightning, he swung his family out of the claws of the roadside transport hustlers. They all let out a deep sigh of relief and rested in the shade as Mr Gregory gave a quick head count of his family. He wasn't about to let a *Home Alone* incident happen to any of his precious chicks.

With gratitude and exceeding joy, the family marched in a single file towards their preferred transport company. Gregory led the team in front, while Felicia was last in the queue to ensure that no one was left behind. They felt like warriors who had just defeated seeming enemies as they beamed with smiles and confirmed their luggage had not been tampered with in any way.

The old man from the crowd that scrambled for passengers kept bothering Gregory. That man should be in his late seventies or thereabouts, he thought. Could he have been a victim of circumstance, foolishness, or greed like me? Now, look at the job a man his age has to do to put food on his table. A man who should be resting at home while enjoying his gratuity and pension is here before 6 a.m., running around like a gazelle and struggling to chase travellers with young lads. Instead of me, Gregory Ipeh, doing such a job with young lads in my old age, I would rather return to my village with my pride and settle as a farmer, he concluded.

Gregory sat with the driver in the front, where there was enough room for his long legs. Above all, sitting there made passengers feel special, as if it were a VIP seat of some sort. A young lady in her National Youth Service (NYSC) uniform was sandwiched between Gregory and the bus driver, having participated in a heated argument before the bus moved off. The young lady had arrived earlier than everyone on the bus and she'd claimed the front seat near the door. When Gregory arrived, she jumped off the bus and signalled for him to move inside, an action that had shocked him to his bone marrow. He expected that common sense should tell the young lady to move in so an older man like himself could sit by the door, but she declined, saying that such an action would be like selling her birthright.

"I no go gree, *oga* (sir). Enter inside, I first, you come," said the furious NYSC lady to Gregory.

"Wonderful! But I be man—how small girl like you go put me for inside?" Gregory raised his shrilled voice.

"Oga, I will not go inside for you. Next time, come very early. Na dis kind of behaviour *oyibo people* (white people), dey call toxic masculinity."

"Hey! English-grammar-girl, wetin concern toxic masculinity with the issue on the ground, eh?" one angry woman asked the NYSC lady, eyeing her from head to toe. From her looks, one could tell she insinuated the NYSC lady was a disrespectful troublemaker for insisting on putting an elder inside while she sat by the door.

"But she came first, sir. All seats are the same—why not show some maturity and move inside?" a young male passenger lent his voice to the lone lady.

"No way! What do you mean, mister man? Not under my watch will that happen on this bus," Felicia said, supporting her husband.

"And why not, madam? She came first. She was here before 5 a.m." The male passenger countered.

"But he is an elder, and a man, too," another voice said.

Different voices talked over each other and continued to give their two cents on the topic.

The middle-aged driver sluggishly called for order while resting his hands on his round pot belly, "E don do o, make una stop noise." While the arguments ensued, he listened carefully as each speaker buttressed their point.

From his records, the young lady was indisputably the first customer to have arrived. Also, she'd indicated her preference to sit by the door a week ago. If Gregory desperately needed to sit by the door, he should have indicated his interest in that seat when he booked with the transport company, and he would have been told of the possibility of having the seat if no other person had paid for it.

However, he was a man and the eldest on the bus. In Nigeria, courtesy demanded that he be accorded some respect. Asking him to sit inside while a little girl young enough to be his daughter guarded him on the outside was unheard of. He had to make his decision. After all, he was the captain of the ship, and whatever he said stood. Anyone who did not like it would need the best of luck to find another bus at that odd time. He hit the bus loudly with his palm to call for attention from the passengers in the back seat, and all eyes fell on him in deaf silence.

"Young lady, this is Nigeria, and you know we accord our elders some respect here. Did you come first? Yes! Did you indicate your interest in the front seat by the door? Yes! But for peace's sake, move in, let the man sit outside and posterity will not forget you in your old age."

"Too much wisdom, driver. Correct guy!" a voice shouted from the back of the bus.

The aggrieved lady was defeated. The driver, who'd penned down her request for a seat choice and witnessed her early arrival, had turned down her request to sit in her rightful position. She swallowed some saliva with a feeling of bitterness bulging in her throat and scooted reluctantly to the middle seat. Gregory entered afterwards and slammed the door, *gbam*!

"Yay...!"

"Finally, the fight is over!"

The passengers on the bus clapped joyfully. Some peacemakers encouraged the lady to cheer up. Others praised Gregory for standing his ground as a man should. It wasn't long before a big argument about gender roles ensued amongst the passengers. Some argued that gender roles were healthy and essential for society and their lack would cause a decline in traditional values. Others argued that all were equal, male or female. "What a man can do, most women can do even better."

"What do you mean by we are all equal?" the driver asked one of the equality advocates. "When wars break out, who do they protect alongside the children? Who goes out there risking their lives to face the enemies?"

"Mr Driver, are you equating this with a war?" the young lad on the bus asked the driver, who was now concentrating on his driving.

The driver looked at the young lad through his rearview mirror, hissed loudly and shook his head. "All these Gen Z children," he muttered softly.

One lady broke the brief silence and asked "But what does my gender really want? One minute, we want a gentleman to pamper us and treat us like queens; another minute, we accuse him of being patriarchal and toxic for doing the same things we crave."

"Stop justifying nonsense, aunty. This lady just got robbed of her paid seat. How is that gentlemanism?" the lad rebuked.

"Thank you, my brother. Your wife will enjoy you," echoed a feminine voice from the back seat.

"But the man was only trying to protect the young lady by shielding her between himself and the driver — how is that a problem?" the lady questioned.

"Stop being a 'pick me' aunty, all for women supporting women. Did that lady look like she needed protection?" the same man countered.

Felicia stood by her husband. She bragged about her girls and how they had been brought up morally. None of them would dare misbehave in public over such a senseless issue.

Akpana listened to each person buttress their view on gender roles, thinking how fascinating the journey would be.

Soon they became tired of arguing and some of them went on their phones to browse through social media. Akpana picked up a novel she had left in her bag and began to read.

As the Cross Lines driver sped past the Lagos-Ibadan Expressway, Felicia signalled her girls by widening her eyes with her thumb and index finger. This was meant to send a message to the sleepy heads on the now quiet bus to stay alert and get accustomed to the route.

The journey became lively again when the bus stopped for the passengers to have lunch, stretch their legs, and use the toilet at Asaba in Delta State. Gregory and Felicia ordered hot wraps of fufu with *ogbono* soup and two bottles of chilled Malt from the busy restaurant patronised by everyday travellers. The girls went for white rice with tomato stew and soft drinks. Only Akpana ordered newspaper-wrapped *suya* from a roadside trader from the north, usually called an *aboki* man. She was weary of letting history repeat itself, but suya was grilled beef with a lot of pepper and aromatic spices that gave the popular Nigerian snack a distinct flavour. She assured herself it would do her tummy well and wouldn't cause her to throw up on the passengers due to motion sickness.

Altogether, the passengers spent about forty-five minutes at the eating place before the driver beckoned them to round up with their activities; the journey ahead was still very long.

****

At precisely 10.40 p.m., Gregory and his family arrived at Bebuagbong village in Obudu. The terrible road conditions with potholes and traffic jams, especially in places like Ore and Onitsha, caused the vehicles to move at the speed of a snail. Some people argued they could eat their lunch and dinner in the same vicinity as far as the congestions on the busy roads were concerned.

Most bus drivers had been smart enough to use village routes to manoeuvre past the chaos, but they were usually greeted by village youths who used roadblocking as a source of income. They blocked the road with old tyres and metal drums as they rallied around the travelling buses that came their way. The bus drivers had to negotiate a fee with the youths before they'd let them move past.

That negotiation was not too different from the kind that happened at police checkpoints between bus drivers and police officers on road duty, who stopped and searched travelling buses while asking the driver, "Anything for the boys?"

Also, the bus had broken down a few times, and the driver stopped by the roadside, either to change the tyres or get the bus to keep moving. Gregory and some of the passengers had dropped from the vehicle to assist the driver in pushing the bus until it was good to start again.

When they finally arrived in Obudu town, the passengers gave a huge sigh of relief. Some Christians thanked Jesus and sang his praises. The driver was also heavily praised for his manoeuvring skills, alertness and route knowledge. For an extra fee, he'd offered to drive a few of them to their respective villages since they had no friends or family available to pick them up that night unless they'd loved spending the night in an open motor park and having their bodies feasted on by mosquitoes. The offer was accepted joyfully.

Gregory and his family were the last passengers to be dropped off. The family of eight counted their luggage and checked that nothing was left behind. They thanked the driver and stretched their bodies from side to side as the excessive luggage on the bus had barely given them enough room for relaxation.

The kids tried to peer into what would become their new home, but the thick darkness formed high walls that blinded them. Felicia quickly turned on her phone's torchlight, but there was only so much it could do. Akpana felt the presence of a gigantic tree standing right in the middle of the compound. She had seen it briefly before the bus driver had driven off to the motor park to have some rest for his next day's journey back to Lagos. She rested her back against it and enjoyed the cool air swooshing quietly back and forth. The atmosphere felt calm and peaceful except for the sound of the dancing tree branches and owls that cooed in the night. She had never heard of owls in the noisy Lagos that never slept at night.

The village had a distinct smell, too, one the kids couldn't really fathom. It was a mixture of cool, minted wind with fermented cassava and perhaps fresh green grass or something else that gave the atmosphere its crispiness, all combined in one soothing aura of peace and tranquillity.

The sound of the bus engine moving off after offloading their luggage awoke many light sleepers who ran out with lit lanterns, candles and torch lights that toned down the thick darkness that greeted the family.

"*Lipeh Ujesu o, Unim ashi o* (We thank, Jesus o. God has done well o)," Ama Agnes, the family's oldest daughter, exclaimed, running from her mud kitchen. She had been waiting tirelessly for the family's triumphant arrival, checking from time to time that the wraps of fufu were still hot in the cooler she kept them in. She danced and danced, moving her waist from left to right and then lifting one leg with her arms, spread out like a peacock opening its wings. She let the leg stay high up for a few minutes while the villagers cheered her dancing skill at her age. Then, she dropped the leg, inched forward to the newly arrived and grabbed little Amokeye in a warm embrace.

"Ah, fine people. Una welcome, o. How the journey, na? Hope everything fine-fine?" she asked, pulling the other children into her arms, too.

The other villagers did the same thing. With their torch lights and lanterns beaming on the children's faces, they touched them indiscriminately, made remarks about their age, height, weight and beauty, and talked about which child looked like which parent or distant relative.

"Where the bus driver, *knor*?" a young boy asked stretching the Bette intensifier 'knor' with a strong accent. "Why the bus driver no leave him engine on so that the light can 'lumate' the place before we comot outside, eh? He leave all of you for darkness. Not nice of him."

The kids chuckled lightly. Some children in the rural area were not fluent in English yet they had an audacious manner of expressing themselves. UD shook her head, feeling gutted. She turned to her mother, who pretended not to notice her glance.

"Don't mind him, my dear. The bus driver insisted on rushing back to town to get some rest, but I know that's not true. He hurried to get some passengers from town coming into the village. That is how most of these drivers make some side money to augment their pay before returning to Lagos," Gregory said, patting the young lad on his back.

"Children, this is your big cousin Ukwudi, the youngest son of your aunty Ama Agnes," Gregory said.

"Una welcome," Ukwudi greeted his cousins.

"Thank you," the girls replied, half asleep.

"So, your name is Ukwudi — do you have plenty money?" little Amokeye asked.

The villagers laughed heartily.

"So, you understand small Bette language. Your ama and apa really try for you. Some children live here for Obudu, but dem no hear come chop," Ukwudi said, applauding his cousin's attempt to understand the local language despite being brought up far away, compared to some kids in the same town who believed the local language was meant only for the villagers.

"Ukwudi, leave your cousins alone with plenty of talk. They just dey come from far journey. Allow them to rest," Ama Agnes cautioned her chatterbox son.

"He is just excited to see his cousins," Felicia said cheerfully.

"You no know Ukwudi. Small parrot. Abeg (please) make we enter house. The children need to rest," Ama Agnes said, making her way into the newly built bungalow belonging to Gregory and his family.

The family observed their new home, and Felicia smiled at its ample space and potential for creative ideas. She thought of growing some fruit and vegetables in the large backyard. She missed farming and had always wanted to plant her own vegetables.

"You look younger and fresher since the last time I saw you," Gregory said, acknowledging his older sister's strength and agility as they moved their boxes into their new home.

"You sure? Me wey waist dey pain? I no dey even go farm like before again."

"Wonderful! You no longer go to the farm due to waist pain? What medication are you taking for it?" Gregory asked.

"My brother, I dey manage am dey go. One Calabar woman here for village, dey help me massage am every morning and night."

Felicia joined the conversation between the two siblings: "Sister, don't worry. I am here now. I will massage that pain off your waist in a few days."

"I trust you, Felicia. Good woman," Ama Agnes replied.

The Great Change

"*Kuku roo koo*," a rooster crowed as early as 4.30 a.m. Soon, another crow sounded in the distance, and then a few others followed, too. For the newly arrived children, this was more than a shock. They had never heard so many roosters crowing noisily. Not long after, she heard some voices with what sounded like aluminium pails, and Akpana suspected the voices with the pails were going to fetch some water. The rooster was, indeed, an alarm clock to have gotten a group of people out of bed to go fetch some water and begin their day. In Lagos, their bedside alarm clock had awoken them at dawn, and when they snoozed the alarm, their mother's voice did the thundering that shook them to consciousness.

Akpana dawdled in her bed for a bit as the day got brighter. She knew her family would have to make many adjustments, and a time would come when they, too, would be expected to join the youths visiting the stream very early in the morning.

Soon, visitors began trooping into their home. "*Kpam-kpam,*" they said, using their mouths to reflect the sound of a knock on the door.

Felicia and Gregory were already sitting in their living room, sorting out their luggage. "Come in," Gregory said.

"Peace be unto this house," Ama Alorye, an old family friend, said as she entered the house with her grandkids, carrying a large basket of food.

There was a joyful noise between the guests and the hosts as they exchanged joyful pleasantries.

"Did you people arrive well?" Ama Alorye asked the family.

"The journey was good, thank God," Felicia said.

It wasn't long before other visitors came in, and there was a roar of laughter and happy pleasantries.

A variety of rice graced the centre table. One family had brought white rice and stew with fish, another jollof rice and turkey, and another fried rice and chicken. Other bowls of rice were similar to these. Akpana could see them all from the half-opened curtain leading to the living room.

Then, the guests began asking for the children: "Are they still sleeping?" they enquired. Akpana could not tell if they were being concerned, nosy or sarcastic. She understood the villagers were very agile and always on their feet, so they considered sleepy heads as being lazy people, but Akpana chose to take it as a form of concern, considering they had travelled many hours the day before, and it was only normal for them to still be in bed at 8 a.m.

"They should be awake by now," Felicia said, screaming each person's name. "Akpana! Udanshi! Atimanu! Beyin! Adeshi! Amokeye! Come and say hello to your relatives that have come to greet us."

Some of the girls grumbled as they rolled out of their beds. This was not a good way to start their lives in the village. They'd wanted more sleep time, but their privacy was invaded from every corner as more people trooped into their home.

"This is Ama Alorye—do you remember her, Adeshi? She was the one that carried you during your first birthday party in Lagos, where she visited her son, Uncle Peter, briefly."

"I don't remember, Ma," Adeshi said.

"Ah ah, what do you mean by you don't remember? You don't remember the woman who carried you when you were crying all over the place and refused to snap any pictures on your first birthday?"

"No, Ma," Adeshi said, frowning.

"But do you remember Uncle Peter in Lagos? The one that used to buy you people chocolates whenever he visited our house?"

"Yes, Ma," Adeshi answered.

"This is Uncle Peter's mother," Felicia concluded, looking pleased with herself, as if she had cracked a code or something.

Adeshi and her sisters greeted Ama Alorye good morning in Bette: "Ama, *wo mor.*"

"Ma wombehar?" she replied their greeting, responding in the usual amusing Bette fashion—if the children were able to wake up. "Ah, ah…you children have grown, o. The last time I was in Lagos, you were still running around with little panties, and now some of you are already taller than me with big oranges on your chests. Felicia, what do you people feed children with in that Lagos that makes them grow so big?"

Everyone laughed cheerfully except the tired children. Most of them felt embarrassed that Ama Alorye had exposed their privacy. Some young boys had heard the gist and chuckled mischievously, which made it even worse for the girls.

The afternoon and evening were no different. More people continued to visit from faraway villages. They all came with baskets of cooked and raw food like yams, rice, bush meats and palm wine for entertainment.

Gregory was already enjoying his new life as he played catch-up with his peers. Felicia listened carefully to advisers telling her which crops to plant and which business ventures might fetch her money while in the village.

The children made many observations. In the village, things were accomplished in a more integrated and participatory manner, with more hands and support. The communal living was very different from that in the big city of Lagos. People ate together on the same plate and exchanged food often. They called each other every morning at cock crow to visit the stream and farmlands. They all waited until everyone had finished their business to return home.

Another good thing about their new home was its ample space. Compared to their two-bedroom house in Lagos, they had an enormous living room with six bedrooms, a massive indoor and outdoor firewood kitchen and an external hut Gregory used as his man cave. The parents shared one bedroom, and only two children shared each room. The other rooms were reserved for guests and storing unused items.

Gregory bought a big refrigerator with some of the money left from the loan he'd collected from the Bebuagbong community in Lagos. The fridge helped store freshly cooked food. The only issue was that there was hardly any source of electricity to power it. For that reason, Gregory bought a medium-sized generator.

When he could not afford to fuel the generator that powered the refrigerator, the family had to rely on heating leftover meals at night and warming them up very early the next day to prevent them from getting sour.

The pressure to continue with city life while in the village was a chore. As much as Gregory wanted his family to live in the comfort they had always known, it ate into his pocket. In the first week of their arrival, he'd bought only bottled water for the family for fear of contracting diarrhoea from the village stream. When this method became unsustainable, he encouraged them to adapt to the village norm of fetching fresh flowing water from the stream in their brown earthen pots that kept the water cool. The newbies had to learn to wake up as early as 5 a.m. to arrive at the stream before most people were even awake. It was a chore that was a big nightmare for them. In Lagos, their family had lived a relatively soft life: water ran from taps in their home, and they never bothered to wake up early to fetch some.

Felicia used some of the money she'd made from the carnival to start a small akara and ogi business in Obudu town, the same as in Lagos. Her target customers were the early birds who left for their farms without having breakfast at home and some private and government workers who worked in Obudu Town. She was beginning to get a foothold as one of the few sellers specialising in the akara and ogi business, as most sellers sold *kiwhua* (moi-moi).

As for Gregory, aside from his newly acquired farmland, where he had already begun to plant yam and cassava seedlings, he'd joined his Age Grade Association in the village and was getting the hang of how they operated in his new environment, observing the bluntness of the villagers as opposed to the meandering and sugar-coating of certain words and circumstances within the Lagos Age Grade Community.

On the first day, he stepped his foot in the village town hall, where their usual meetings were held, he was confronted by members of his Age Grade. "Gregory, based on our records, you owe us some money," said the *akawu* (secretary), a smallish, slender man in his early fifties, flipping through endless pages as he glanced at Gregory over the top end of his glasses. Gregory was not surprised that, for the first time since his arrival in the village, someone had finally pronounced his name like the British officers he had worked with at the NRC. Others pronounced his name as 'Grigori' rather than the posh way the English speakers called him 'Gregri'. The akawu was one of the few men in his days who had been fortunate enough to be sponsored by some Catholic missionaries to further his education in Canada. Upon graduation, he returned from the university and refused to work for anybody. Instead, he established his own secondary school and was the sole administrator until his retirement a few years ago, when he handed over the administration of his school to his daughter. Since then, his Age Grade entrusted him with the responsibility of being their akawu.

"Wonderful! What do you mean by I owe the group some money? I paid in Lagos, where I resided for a good thirty years," a furious Gregory, who was running out of cash, retorted.

"Gregory, the one you paid was for the Lagos people. To be a part of us here in the village, you must pay the levy that we all paid for the funeral of Augustus, our brother, who died mysteriously six years ago. You must also pay for William and Ikpali's wedding, plus our monthly contribution of two-hundred naira. All these are backdated to just two years ago to make it easier for you," the akawu said.

"And where shall I get all that money you are quoting and quoting from? Didn't you hear what happened to me from my sojourn in the big man's city?" Gregory asked.

"Let me come in, Gregory and Akawu," the president of the Age Grade cut in. "We always write letters informing you Lagos people of the Age Grade levy here in the village, but you people over there always insist on having a different territory from us. That is how Ashiwel buried his aged father in Lagos. He refused to come back home to perform the traditional rites and customs of our people, claiming that he was now a born-again Christian and wouldn't want to do certain rituals here with us. He claimed that the Bebuagbong community in Lagos had collected a few kegs of palm wine and kola nuts on our behalf and given him the go-ahead to bury a whole Ukandi (elder) Adie in the strange land of Lagos far away from his ancestors. Can you imagine that?"

"God forbid," a voice yelled.

"Our forefathers will be turning in their graves," another elder interjected.

"When did such new-age madness start?" the president continued. "The village is the bedrock of our community, and every activity must return to its root for the authenti… authenti—"

"Authentication of events," the akawu helped the struggling president.

"Thank you, Akawu," the president said. "The only way we get you people to follow protocol is when one of you returns home like you have just done. So, as the president of this noble association, I say to you, Gregory Ipeh, that you must pay all backdated levies to be recognised as our member here in the village, *shikena* (period)."

"Wonderful. This is a conspiracy! This is preposterous! This is unacceptable! This is—"

"Gregory! This is not Lagos. All those big-big grammar you are blowing will not wriggle you out of this situation. Our president has spoken, and that is that," an elder from the group of men concurred.

Like a frozen chicken with its wings tied between its thighs, Gregory sat dumbfounded on the white plastic chair in the village town hall, so different from the one they used for their meetings in Lagos. If the meeting had moved on to a different topic, he wasn't aware.

Being a member of the Age Grade Association had its benefits. You had a group to fall back on during all forms of disputes including land, farm and family issues, also financial intervention in the case of any unfortunate events. However, he had a lot on his plate. A backdated payment to the Age Grade Association was an additional financial strain, plus the interest loan to be repaid to the Bebuagbong community in Lagos. Most of all, the new wife he planned to marry from Kakum, a neighbouring village, to produce an heir.

A New Wife

The prevalent cultural issue of preferring sons to daughters has stood the test of time in many nations of the world. In these societies, a male child was the one who succeeded his father and continued the family lineage by inheritance. They were seen as protectors and defenders of their fathers' households, but not so for the daughters, who, though considered beautiful and a blessing, were seen as second fiddle to their male counterparts.

For many families, the joy of a daughter was usually considered a blessing because of the huge bride price they hoped to receive from prospective sons-in-law in the future, and the idea that women could one day become governors' or presidents' wives rather than being in those positions themselves. More so, a woman's nurturing tendencies came in handy in her parents' old age. Aside from these facts, she was considered not as useful in matters of inheritance, succession and continuing the family name, as many women marry and adopt the surname of their husband.

Gregory shared these sentiments even though he was enlightened enough to see how well women succeeded in the city of Lagos. However, sometimes, cultural biases eat deep into people's sub consciousnesses. The thought of his name dying with him bothered him a lot. For many years in Lagos, he either avoided phone calls that toed that line of conversation or laughed over the topic when caught off guard. However, his presence in the village made way for straight conversations about not having a son. His peers at his Age Grade meetings playfully remarked about who would succeed him. Sometimes, they teased him about the fragility of his daughters while working on his farmland, how they looked like they could collapse any minute and how their sons had done twice the work the girls were still doing.

"Gregory, this house of yours is quite impressive, you know, but who will inherit it after you have gone to meet with your ancestors?" one man had asked him while moving a black piece on the draught board during one of their games. "You know your daughters will all be married soon and belong to another family, leaving your household empty, with only Felicia managing your home."

Gregory imagined another man starting a relationship with his wife under his roof after his demise. He shook the thought from his mind, but the little talks trickled in and began to gain ground in his vulnerable mind.

Gregory made up his mind to marry a second wife. She would do the magic and bear him a son to continue his lineage and stand in as the 'man of the house' in his absence. The young wife would also keep him looking fresh and young from the fountain of her youthfulness. As for Felicia, she wouldn't be the first woman whose husband had taken a second wife, and he believed she would adapt and understand the bigger picture as time went on.

The fact that Gregory might be responsible for the sex of his children was a piece of alien news to him and ninety-nine others. In many cultures, the woman was to blame when the children were females.

However, if the child was a boy, the man was praised and validated as a 'strong man.'

Ikel was the young girl Gregory planned to marry. She was a Federal College of Education graduate in her twenties, and there was no doubt her womb would do its magic.

Judging from her humble background, Gregory believed Ikel would be loyal and submissive to him. He admired her beautiful altar decorations as one of the proud members of the Mary League Society in Saint Theresa the Little Flower Catholic Church. Most of all, she wasn't jobless. She worked as a primary school teacher, which scored high in his 'wife material' search.

Gregory paid her bride price, promising her single mother to love and cherish his young bride till his dying day.

Felicia had to accept her reality. Gregory had told her of his plans a week before paying Ikel's bride price. She'd smiled softly and said words of peace: "It's okay."

****

Many months had gone by since Ikel joined her new family. Despite the duration of her stay, she and her co-wife never saw eye to-eye. Felicia found it humiliating to share her husband with a small girl like Ikel, who was already expecting her first child. Sadly, her husband spent more nights in the guest room where Ikel had settled than in their master bedroom. He claimed Ikel's blood was still very cold, and he needed to be by her side for warmth or risk the young lady looking elsewhere for satisfaction. Both Ikel and Gregory cackled annoyingly, like baby hyenas, over little nothings on the bouncy spring bed in the guest room. On some days, they ran around the house like little children, playing hide and seek, and Felicia worried about destroying her children's innocence, so she would instruct them to retire to bed early and keep their doors tightly shut till the next morning.

"Ahhhh…I remember the good old days when Gregory was still Gregory, very strong and capable," she exclaimed to herself one night, biting her lower lip upon hearing a big tussle that surprisingly quietened before she could finish soliloquising. She burst into a barking laughter, chiming like broken glass as she sieved through the deafening silence after a few minutes of 'rumpy-pumpy'.

"Is that it?" she questioned loudly, still booming with laughter that echoed beyond their divided wall. Gregory was now an old man; nothing lasted forever. Although the poor man would never admit that he was losing strength below—he either blamed his inactivity on stress or excess sugar from Felicia's ogi.

Ikel enjoyed taunting Felicia, especially with fake sounds of pleasure, knowing that a wall was the only separation she had between her and her rival, who, though she dwelt in the big master bedroom, only kept warm with a pile of pillows soaked in misery and lack of affection.

Felicia could swear Ikel faked her sounds of pleasure to well up envy within her, but she didn't let that bother her too much. As far as she was concerned, Ikel was feasting on her leftovers like a vulture scavenging on remains.

Felicia chose to endure the excesses of the man she had suffered with for many years in Lagos and stood by despite his gross misconduct at the Nigerian Railway Corporation, a man with whom she had bore six beautiful, intelligent and hardworking daughters, but Gregory had rubbed sand-sand on all of that because he sought a male child.

One hot afternoon, Felicia had just returned from her daily akara and ogi sale. She looked exhausted, but as usual, she had a positive outlook. A closer look at her under the radiating sun would reveal that she was beginning to age, with a few grey hairs here and there, but Felicia was a natural beauty. She still looked well kept, especially as she was now trying to keep up with a younger wife.

Ikel sighted Felicia through her bedroom window, facing one of the entrances to the family house, and jumped out of her spring bed with her pregnancy bump nearly reaching her thighs. She grabbed the nearest wrapper and wrapped it hurriedly around her waist. As soon as Felicia had set foot into the family compound, Ikel started singing loudly:

"Some people jealous me, some people jealous me,
some people jealous me because of my beauty.
I will not mind them, I will not mind them,
I will not mind them because they are ugly."

Felicia felt insulted. "Come, Ikel—who are the 'some people' you refer to in that your *yeye* (nonsense) song?" she asked.

"Guilty conscience—did I call anybody's name?" Ikel retorted.

"May thunder fire that mouth that you use to insult me with, you silly rabbit! If not for Gregory, who belittled me by bringing a scarecrow like you to our matrimonial home, where would you have sighted even my shadow in the same space with you? You wouldn't even inhale the same air that I breathe, you mannerless child!"

"Every time: manners! Manners! Manners! Do you eat manners, Felicia? You are just jealous of my presence in this house. Admit it, and shame the devil."

Felicia laughed hysterically. "Me, Felicia? Jealous of you? I laugh in Spanish. If you think you measure up to me, you'd better think twice. Just take a good look at me," Felicia said, turning clockwise and anticlockwise to show off her well-structured feminine physique. "A mother of six—look at how sumptuous I look at my age, but who can say the same about you in your twenties, looking like an overfed cow," Felicia said with a smirk.

"Yen, yen, yen—whatever, Felicia. After all, our husband prefers to spend more nights with an over-fed cow than a dry wood. Doesn't that tell you something, Madam Sumptuous?" Ikel said.

Felicia shook her head softly and kissed her teeth. "You know what our elders say?" she asked Ikel. "The new broom might sweep clean, but only the old broom knows the nooks and crannies. Now, listen to me, young girl, I am not your mate, so I cannot be seen trading words with you, but let me tell you, in case your coconut head is not aware: I was married into this family many years ago, honourably, with my dignity and pride, wedded in the Roman Catholic Church and welcomed by the Catholic Women Organisation of

Nigeria with open arms." Felicia illustrated this by spreading her arms like a proud peacock. "I didn't go through the back door like you, a church worker who got pregnant outside wedlock by a married man. So, tell me again, between you and me, who should be jealous of whom?"

Ikel welled up with anger. If she were a dragon, she could have spat out fire, but the heat in her mouth was stuffed in her puffy cheeks with her buttoned nose rising and falling. She advanced towards Felicia without thinking it through and raised her hand to Felicia's cheek.

"Not on your life!" Felicia warned, catching Ikel's chubby hand before it met with her cheek.

"Ahhh… Poor thing." Felicia sighed. "It must really hurt, doesn't it?" she asked. "A young girl like you with no church wedding, no Mary League send-off, no more holy communion during masses, nothing. You are just an unfortunate baby-making machine for a desperate man old enough to be your father who is willing to feed your empty stomach and that of your wretched family. That's all you are."

Ikel pulled her hand free of Felicia's firm grip. Tears began falling like raindrops from her bulging eyes. Her mate had struck many chords. When it came to verbal exchange, leave it to Felicia. She had the upper hand. Her tongue was as sharp as a razor blade despite her calm appearance. Some people called her the Silent Thunder. Her speech was a venom that had no antidote. This time, it infused into Ikel, leaving her scarred.

However, Ikel knew her mate was right. She had come into the family through the back door, but rubbing it on her face because of a little argument had been uncalled for. Ikel stood there in burning anger, eyeing Felicia with her arms akimbo, her foot tapping aggressively on the red earthen soil. She bit her index finger and wiped it furiously through the air with a scheme for dealing with Felicia popping into her mind. She would do what she knew how to do best, which was to incriminate her victim and appear to be innocent herself.

For no reason, Ikel began to leap like a frog in the air despite how far gone her pregnancy was. She called for assistance like a child who had just been flogged with a cane. The thought of her late father aided the downpour of tears to validate her grievance. "*Ma beh o; Felicia ula gwam o* (People come to my aid; Felicia wants to kill me o)!" Ikel ran around the compound, screaming at the top of her voice until she saw people approaching the scene. She dropped to the ground with her baby bump in the middle of her widely parted legs, yelling, "What is my offence that she beats me like a thief caught in the marketplace?" She placed her hands on her head, and crocodile tears continued to drop down her eyes.

"What is the matter, these women? Can't a man have some peace in his own house?" Gregory yelled, rushing to the backyard with his wrapper tied loosely to his waist. He had just returned from playing draught with his mates when he'd heard his pregnant wife's screams.

"Felicia, have I offended you in any way? Why do you want to hurt this little girl, old enough to be your daughter, eh?" Gregory asked.

"Is that it, Gregory Ipeh? You come in here and blame me without first asking questions?"

"I do not need any interview to understand the situation, Felicia. Be gentle with your co-wife — is that too much for a man to ask of his wife? Even a blind man can see that she is heavily pregnant, for goodness' sake, Felicia."

"It's all right, Gregory. Take sides, as always. God knows best. I leave you all to him." Felicia stomped out of the scene disheartened, banging and hitting anything that stood her way. Some neighbours had lingered long enough to grab the gist of the latest episode of the Gregory household family feud.

Gregory lifted his heavily pregnant wife from the floor. She had rubbed sand all over her sweaty body to exaggerate the situation. He used the edge of his wrapper to wipe her sandy body clean and then ushered her to the bathroom.

"Atimanu!" Gregory called out to his daughter.

"Yes, Daddy?"

"Fetch a bucket of water for your second mother to bathe quickly."

"Yes, sir," she replied, running off to the big red aluminium drum in their backyard, which the kids filled with water every morning, making several trips to the stream.

Atimanu used a round plastic bowl to scoop water into a pail and made her way to their outdoor cubicle bathroom.

Due to the advancement of Ikel's pregnancy, she had ditched the comfort of their indoor bathroom, preferring the refreshing feeling of bathing in their palm frond and bamboo-fenced bathroom, usually covered with a towel or wrapper for privacy. She loved the minty air from the surrounding trees blowing on her skin while standing on a sunken-slabbed patio and scooping the cool water from the pail onto her body.

Felicia watched helplessly as her daughter served the woman who had caused her grief. With her naked eyes, she had seen the man she loved and stood by drift into the arms of another woman in pursuit of a son. Men are fascinating characters, she thought. She cursed her stars and, in her heart, blamed God for not giving her a boy-child. She remembered her high hopes before the conception of her last daughter, Amokeye.

Pastor Lazarus of the Church of Harvest of Bliss and Plenty had assured her that everything was possible with faith. He had read Bible passages to her illustrating the faith of Abraham, who'd had a child with his wife, Sarah, at an old age, and Hannah, who'd prayed like a mad drunk at Shiloh. God had heard and blessed her with Samuel. "If only your faith was as small as a mustard seed, you would move mountains," he'd say to her. So, with unwavering faith, she'd gotten pregnant again, never doubting at any point the possibility of having a son. Felicia had sown a seed of faith with her widow's mite to support the church projects and bought boys' clothes and shoes. All the baby blankets and overalls were blue and grey. She told her girls and boasted to Gregory that her 'sonshine' was on the way.

Nine months had gone by, and it was time for Felicia to prove a point. It was still early in the morning when the cramps of labour started. Being experienced, Felicia prepared her maternity bag and left for the hospital a few miles away from their house. The midwives saw her condition and quickly admitted her to the maternity ward to monitor the procedure. When the time of delivery came, they encouraged the expectant mother to push her unborn child out. It wasn't too long before Felicia delivered the baby safely.

"Congratulations, madam — it's a beautiful baby girl," one of the midwives said to her, smiling from ear to ear. You should have seen the shock on Felicia's face upon hearing the words that struck her heart like lightning.

The bombshell revelation had made her spread her baby's legs apart to confirm what her ears had just received. *Hah!* God played me, she blasphemed. Now, what was she to do with a child whose gender she dreaded having again? She knew she loved the child, but she hated what was between her legs. So, she wailed and screamed in the hospital, refusing to breastfeed her baby despite the pleas of the midwives. She thought about the numerous pieces of advice from well-meaning family, friends and Christians, asking her to try again for a different gender as if they knew she would surely have a son, but the problem with these advisers was that they never told the newly delivered mother what to do with the baby when she got the opposite of what she hoped for: throw the child away or accept the child as being what they call God's will?

Felicia felt devastated and overwhelmed, which led to severe post-partum depression. She wouldn't touch the child, nor would she breastfeed her. Worst of all, the cries of the baby ached Felicia's ears so badly she'd once threatened to throw the baby off a bridge. Gregory had to seek help from friends and family to guard the child closely, or his wife might shock the world with a piece of breaking news.

After months had passed without naming the child, Felicia finally wiped her tears and looked at her baby girl as she lay in the old wooden crib her sisters had used before her. She was the prettiest little thing she had ever seen, even though it took her so long to see that. She picked up the baby with love in her swollen eyes and named her *Bemokuke-Unimye* (loosely pronounced as 'Amokeye'), which means that—God's gift cannot be rejected.

A Larger Family

It was a dry Saturday afternoon. The sun was blazing over the hills of Obudu like it was no man's business, creating mirage images on the partially tarred roads. Sweaty farmers sat underneath a huge iroko tree that shielded them from the scorching sun, fanning themselves with hand fans that had been nicely woven by skilled weavers from Northern-Nigeria.

A young lad covered in smoke was bent over, flipping sliced yams that had been placed on logs of lit firewood to be roasted. The yams were to be eaten with salted palm oil and pepper. The farmers had been tilling and planting yam seedlings on huge hectares of land all morning, and a quick meal like that would replenish their strength before returning home to a properly home-cooked meal.

As they waited for their yams to roast, they laughed loudly and chatted about their last *bipam bifefe* (New Yam)

Festival and how Udida was very deserving of his recognition as farmer of the year compared to the other farmers. They bet amongst themselves who would take the title in the coming bipam bifefe competition.

Gregory had assured his peers that he would one day win the title, but the big roar after he had spoken made him question why his farming abilities were doubted.

"How many sons have you got to till the land and plant yam seedlings, eh, Gregory? Do you think competitors of the bipam bifefe come there to play?" Adie, a fellow farmer, asked Gregory.

"Don't mind Gregory. He probably thinks it's a beauty pageant competition or something," Paul, another farmer, chimed in.

The men laughed at the beauty pageant joke, but Gregory refused to join in, fixing his gaze at a distance. The men carried on, chatting loudly about how farming was a man's job, while the women did better with cooking and serving the meals.

Gregory remained silent, watching the young lad divide the roasted yams into halves in a big bowl. He served it to the farmers with some palm oil from a congealed palm oil gallon that had been heated across the fire to loosen it up for a free flow.

"*Woshi o*," they thanked him and pounced on the meal like hungry lions.

It didn't take long after the men began enjoying their meal for the overbearing vitamin D of the scorching sun to be quenched by a drizzle. The bare-chested farmers gave a huge sigh of relief. Back in the day, the combination of sunlight and rain was believed to be a sign that an elephant was having its baby.

"Uncle, uncle," a young voice called a now tired Gregory, who was eating some hot roasted yams with palm oil. "The midwife say I should call you," the young boy said.

"Midwife? Is Ikel having the baby now?" Gregory asked, his eyes opened in excitement while he chewed on a dancing piece of yam that was smoking from his mouth. "I no know uncle. She just say make I call you to come quick-quick."

"Come, quick-quick?" Gregory repeated, not knowing what to make of the urgent call. Was Ikel having their baby peacefully, or was there a complication? Did he have to arrange for transportation to Dr Ahmed's clinic in town, where Ikel had been attending her antenatal care, or was it something the midwife could handle? An array of thoughts beclouded the ageing man as he hopped two steps behind the young chap along the bush tracks back to his house.

Gregory heard a loud noise from a distance and suspected the joyous atmosphere was booming from his compound. Ikel must have delivered their child, he thought as his heart skipped a beat. What might the sex of the child be? If only the scanning machine had been working properly at the clinic, the sex of the child would have been known a long time ago to prepare his heart for what was to come. However, each time Ikel visited the clinic, the sonographer complained of being unable to tell the gender due to some fault with the machine.

Gregory listened carefully to hear what his itching ears desired. However, the voices speaking loudly in his compound didn't give the sex of the baby away, but the ululating he heard was certainly a sign that the child had been born already, and Ikel had proven herself to be the strong woman he always believed her to be.

Back in his compound, the air was filled with an array of emotions. Some people shed a few tears, overwhelmed with exceeding joy, while others were in total awe of what a woman's body could do. Ikel was still lying on the brown and pink raffia mat spread out on the cemented floor, her head supported by a pillow and her body covered with a blood-stained piece of wrapper. The young woman was weak but strengthened by the cries of her newborn. A few hours ago, she had been in excruciating pain from the contractions tightening her womb like the crushing of a can, but all that was in the past now.

The midwife and her assistants cleaned up mum and baby and transferred them to Ikel's spring-bed mattress to recuperate. There was a lot of singing, dancing, and praising

God. This jubilation and doxology attracted passers-by, who stopped to join in the happy moment.

Gregory stepped into his large compound, his curiosity moving his wobbly feet even faster as if he were floating in the air. Given the beaming faces hanging under the avocado tree by his house, he suspected it must be the desired news.

"Una, well done, o!" He saluted the women who'd assisted in the delivery. They began ululating upon seeing him and sprinkled cans of baby powder carelessly on his face and body, which was the usual way of greeting a new parent.

Gregory gave them little attention. His full gaze was on the child, trying to peek into its sex area.

Ikel cut quickly to the chase. "It's a boy!"

"What did you say, *udim* (love)?"

"It's a baby boy, my husband."

Gregory let out a big scream that left people laughing as they waited for his reaction to the news.

"Wonderful! Wonderful! My God has done me well. Wonderful!" he screamed. Turning to Ikel, he said, "Udim, you have honoured me. You have made me a complete man!"

The new dad dropped his farm tools on the cemented floor, wiped his hands on his brown khaki shorts and collected the baby from the arms of his exhausted mother. He stared deeply into his son's eyes with gratitude and exceeding joy. "At last, a man like me. The strength of my manhood.

My heir apparent." He smiled, cuddled the baby, and spoke blessings in a muffled tone.

"You shall rule, my boy. You are a star. Nations shall rise to honour you. No weapon formed against you shall prosper. Ah! He has your nose, Ikel, but his lips and chubby cheeks are mine."

Gregory's happiness made Ikel feel very proud of herself, like she had won a trophy of some sort. She knew the little one with a weenie was the principal reason she had been invited into Gregory Ipeh's family. Now that she'd bore an heir, she could relax with her two legs spread apart and watch the world drop at her feet.

"What do you think of the name, Utsu?" Gregory asked Ikel.

"Utsu is good," she replied, half asleep.

"Then Utsu, it is because indeed he is king."

The hilarity of the news had spread across the neighbouring towns and villages. Even those in faraway Lagos received phone calls that Gregory Ipeh had finally fathered a son in his old age.

Gregory's farmer friends, who heard the news on their way home, rejoiced on his behalf.

Hunters carrying dead deer and bush rabbits they'd caught for food and trade heard gossipers talking about the latest update in the village as they hung idly around the bush tracks. The hunters shared in the joy of the news and promised to share their game with the father of a bouncing new baby boy.

Felicia heard the news while she was rounding off her market sales. Many women came specifically to congratulate her on the birth of her stepson. They looked straight into her eyes as if searching her soul for signs of jealousy or wishful thoughts, but Felicia was wise; she smiled and leapt for joy as each one came, dancing and twirling unexpectedly around.

Soon, it was time to retire from her daily sales, but she'd rather sleep in the market than go home and see the victory in Ikel's eyes. She dragged her feet reluctantly, moving from stall to stall with an empty ogi cooler and akara tray. Felicia shivered with goosebumps crawling out of her melanised skin despite the scorching sun that had now risen after winning its fight with the invading rain showers.

She thought of a few other things to buy. "I think I will check for new school uniform material for Amokeye and Atimanu before the next session," she said to herself. "I could also check for a new bedspread and slippers for myself," she muttered quietly, moving from shop to shop, buying unnecessary materials. Soon, her tired feet could no longer continue the roundabout journey, so she mustered the courage to return home.

"What is this heart-aching feeling?" she asked herself. Was it envy that another woman had come from nowhere to do what she'd tried to do six good times and failed?

Was it overwhelming joy that their family finally had the missing piece to their dynamic structure? Perhaps it was the fear of a disrespectful Ikel taunting her or the fear of other people concluding that she, Felicia, was responsible for the release of the sex cells that had brought their six daughters into existence. Deep in her heart, she hoped God would reprimand the proud Ikel by giving her a set of twin girls. Then, she would laugh at her husband and the side piece he'd brought to their matrimonial home. *Chai!* But God's ways are not man's, so she would have to face her fears with her head high. She did a lot of breathing exercises and practised smiling as she walked from Obudu Market to Bebuagbong village, carrying her purchased materials as if they weighed nothing. She usually used a commercial motorcycle to ease the stress of walking home after a stressful sales day, but not that day. She was in no hurry at all.

****

Utsu, Ikel's first son, was only eleven months old when his younger brother was born. The villagers threw a big party for Gregory, registering the birth of his second son as a seal that his lineage would never be lost. Gregory and Ikel named their second son Lipeunim, a Bette name that means "We thank God".

At that point, Felicia was inspired to try for the seventh time before menopause stopped her shine. From the look of things, Gregory's chromosomal swimmers were beginning to behave themselves and release the desired Y chromosomes, so she'd better jump in and get her share before they reverted to their default setting.

After weeks of pondering and strategic planning, Felicia made sure to have Gregory in her bed at certain times of each month until her plan had materialised. Gregory smelled a rat and wondered about Felicia's sudden generous affection towards him after a long absence of quality intimacy, but Felicia assured him that all was well, and she missed the times they shared together as man and wife over senseless arguments and family troubles.

It didn't take long before Felicia's shooting tummy exposed her schemes. This revelation caused a big rift between her and her husband. He couldn't believe his wife had the temerity to add another mouth to feed to their struggling family.

As her pregnancy progressed, the laughable tale Felicia had told about excessive fufu causing her tummy to swell caused the village jesters to get to work. Since then, people jokingly asked pregnant women if they'd eaten too much fufu that caused their tummies to bulge.

Ikel most times burst into rhythmless songs about a woman who tried to change her destiny by any means necessary but failed time and time again because it was never in the books for her.

Gregory stopped eating Felicia's food and called her a dangerous woman who was capable of poisoning his meal. Not even his dear sister Ama Agnes could reconcile the broken bond the new pregnancy caused between the couple.

People accused Felicia of trying to compete with her younger mate despite her age and how sneaky she was about it to the disapproval of her husband.

So, Felicia hung onto the outcome of her last pregnancy by a thread, enduring mockery from every Tom, Dick and Harry that she sometimes wondered if it had been worth it to try again.

On one peaceful night, while men slept and rested from their daily hustling and bustling, mercy said, "Yes, it was worth it to try again." The little, brown-eyed baby Felicia had popped out was the missing star that cleared her dark skies. He was like a coat in winter, like joy in the morning. The midwife ululated that night as Felicia clung tightly to her baby boy as though she feared he might be snatched from her arms. Her heart was full, and her joy was complete.

Without hesitation, she named him Unimke, which means "God's gift," and everyone who came to see her on that night called the child by his name.

Jangilova — Epo-Motor

It was getting towards the end of the year, and the Obudu people had begun to feel the cold, dry Harmattan breeze blasting through the Obanliku Mountains down to the valley dwellers of the Obudu town and villages. The massive strength of the dust-laden wind was felt as it chapped lips and sucked up moisture from the skin of every human being alive. It was a time when some people claimed they could separate the clean lads and lasses from the unkempt ones by simply looking at their Vaseline-malnourished lips or dusty white feet that were suffering from the gush of dry dust bombarding the whole of West Africa from the Sahara Desert.

The usually green vegetation of the thick forest in that rural area seized the opportunity to shine. An aerial view from a distance would display a colourful mix of brownish, bright yellowish, and orange-coloured leaves hanging on branches, waiting to be added to the pile of dried leaves on the ground. During peak cold Harmattan days, these dried leaves were used as fuel for open fires that warmed the people early in the morning and late at night, as well as aiding the fast cooking of outdoor firewood meals.

More prevalently, the Harmattan-dried leaves served as playthings for many children in rural communities, who requested for two strong people to lift them up in the air, with one person holding tightly to their arms and the other holding tightly to their legs and swing them from side to side to the rhythm and response of the song "*Jangilova!*—*Epo-motor!* Jangilova!—Epo-motor!" They sang the Nigerian version of 'Jingle Over like a Motor', until they were eventually dumped into the pile of dried maple leaves while their peers roared in laughter.

On that day, a long queue of children pleaded to be swung and dumped into the pile.

"I don tire for this una everyday jangilova," Ukwudi had told them, but they kept on pleading with him to do jangilova with them.

"Okay. Only one round each. After that one round, una go leave me to rest?"

"Yes, uncle," the children chorused, promising to let Ukwudi be after a round of swing and fling.

Ukwudi and a teenage girl began the activity with the children, chorusing the swing song: "Jangilova!—Epo-motor!

Jangilova!—Epo-motor!" They roared in laughter every time someone was dumped in the pile and watched, amused as they struggled to make their way out.

Soon, it was Unimke's turn. The four-year-old lifted his arms to be carried while giggling in excitement. The other children began to sing the jangilova song again.

Although, being dropped into the pile was like a stone sinking underwater, the children made their way out in a few seconds while giggling from the fun of the activity. Surprisingly, Unimke didn't immediately pop his head out as the other children had after landing in it.

"Unimke! Unimke! Where are you?" exclaimed an anxious Ukwudi, scrambling around in the pile of leaves, not sure of the exact spot he had flung the child to. He became restless and mumbled to himself, "And I refuse to play before, o. Why I no listen to my mind, eh? This boy want to put me for trouble today."

Occasionally, kids got lost in the pile of leaves, so it wasn't anything to panic about. However, Unimke was a different breed. He was not a regular child with a regular mother. For the third time in less than ten minutes, Felicia had come out of their family's kitchen, stretching her giraffe-like neck to ensure her baby boy was still in sight.

The boy was practically his mother's egg that was not to be held loosely or he'd crush. Unimke shut the mouths of her enemies and gave her the confidence she desired in her marital home. For that reason, she treasured him and watched over him like a hawk.

"Peekaboo!" came a tiny voice from the pile.

"You fear me, Unimke. Why you stay inside there for long, eh?" asked Ukwudi, who was still trying to recover from the thought of being pounced on by Felicia over the disappearance of her golden child. One time, Lipeunim, Unimke's half-brother, mistakenly hit him in his left eye with a football while they were running around pretending to be Messi and Ronaldo. Felicia had rained fire and brimstone not only on little Lipeunim but on Ikel, Lipeunim's innocent mother, as well.

Everyone knew Unimke was never to be toyed with, or didn't Ikel and her sons get the memo? By the way, hadn't the same Ikel given a funny chuckle many years ago when one of the ladies in the market had referred to her as an 'unsettled woman'? One would have thought that a co-wife would stand up to a bully like Agatha and defend her mate when such names were heaped on her head in public, but Ikel chuckled instead, making her equally guilty of the offence. That mockery had given Felicia the final push to try one last time for the bull's eye. Now that the good Lord had blessed her womb with Unimke, Ikel had sent her evil son to blind her pride's left eye with a hard football in the name of playing games. It had taken their husband and two other elders in the village to settle the co-wives. Since that altercation, anyone who played with Unimke knew to play cautiously.

"I no go play again. This Unimke disappearance na big sign to stop playing for today," Ukwudi said to the other children waiting their turn in the queue.

"Oh, no! Uncle, please nau, uncle, please," they begged to have their turn before he retired for the day, but the young lad was too shaken to continue.

Soon, they all resigned to fate, dispelling from the heap one after the other, observing that Ukwudi would not budge. They slowly integrated into the other games played around them. Some of them ran around as ball boys for the older boys playing football with two narrow goalposts called monkey posts.

A hair braider sat close by, listening to a small radio that hung by a window while preparing to braid her client's hair. Some of the children roaming around joined them. They volunteered to help section out strands of hair attachments that would be braided into the natural hair of the young girl with an afro hair seated in front of her.

"Give me small-small attachment, first and then medium size, and then big-big," the braider told her helpers.

"Aunty, is it Ghana weaving hairstyle that you want to make?" one of the young girls asked.

"You are correct, my dear. If you put your eyes well-well, you will learn to do hair like me and earn clean money when you grow up instead of wasting your time to play jangilova."

Meanwhile, UD, the second daughter of Gregory and Felicia, sat by the narrow corridor leading to their firewood kitchen. From there, she watched the activities absentmindedly. Though her gaze was on the children playing, her mind had travelled many kilometres away. She had just rounded off from university with a degree in Elementary Education, but she wasn't thrilled about schooling children at the elementary level. The young kids in her family were enough headache, and working in a similar environment would drive her nuts. Getting a slot in the *Big Brother Nigeria* house seemed more like a dream, as was becoming a famous Instagram model or even a popular tiktoker with many followers, comments and likes. Firstly, she needed the latest model of an iPhone to take good photographs and videos, a luxury she couldn't afford yet.

Her mind drifted elsewhere to the light-skinned Bambeshi, who had asked her to be his girlfriend with the view of getting married. She'd said yes to him. The only issue was that Bambeshi had not yet secured a job after his National Youth Service. Regardless of his joblessness, the young man was confident in himself and very reassuring. "I promise I'll find a job. I'll look after you and treat you like the queen that you are," he'd told her in one of his visits to her students' hostel.

Bambeshi had a way with words. His voice was as smooth as butter. With it, he could soften the most formidable lady alive. He knew how to say things UD loved to hear. All he had to do was stare at her with his sleepy eyes while speaking in a soft, soothing tone that captured her entire existence, and he had her full attention. However, what use was it walking into the future with a broke bloke? She wondered if love would pay the bills or feed the family. And what would happen when the babies started coming? God forbid that she gives birth to children in abject poverty and misery.

Though it was the dream of many young girls her age to wear a long white wedding dress with a veil as they walked down the aisle in slow motion to the tune of "Here Comes the Bride", it certainly was not with a man still trying to find his feet.

"UD," Gregory called to his daughter, who was lost in thought as she pulled the end of the wrapper around her waist, twirling and unwinding it around her index finger repeatedly.

"Udanshi," he called out the second time.

"Yes, Daddy?" She jolted back to consciousness upon hearing her full name. Everyone called her UD and only called out her full name when there was trouble lurking.

"Do you want to ruin your mother's wrapper with the way you are squeezing it? Besides, what was that beam I saw on your face?"

"Nothing, sir. I remembered something," UD answered, her left eye twitching.

"Wonderful! Your name might mean clever, but you must remember that the apple doesn't fall far from the tree. You better get that mischievous smile off your face and tell any man that is interested in you that he must come and see your father, as a man should," Gregory warned. "No hanky-panky in my house, o. Worst of all, if you ever get pregnant out of wedlock, I will push you to the man responsible for free. You know what I can do," he warned further.

"My daughters are very responsible. I raised them right," Felicia interjected from the bedroom.

"You raised them right, indeed," Gregory replied. "You should have seen the silly smile on her face when I walked in on her to confirm how responsible she really is."

The other children eavesdropped on the conversation in pin-drop silence, chuckling and whispering into each other's ears. Many of these children had seen UD frolicking with a few brothers in the village. They knew her rugged movement, and the news of her engagements had passed through the ears and lips of the villagers.

One thing about living in the village community was that one person's business was usually everybody's business. That went either positively or negatively. For example, suppose a brother or a sister were ill and unable to call for assistance. There was always the chance that a friend or family member could knock on their door to check that all was well with them, having not seen them for the day. They would raise the alarm if they got no response and break the door before professional services arrived. The communal life also made it possible for those in whatever kind of need, whether service or provisional, to get assistance.

In contrast, families found it almost impossible to keep their businesses and domestic issues within the four walls of their households. If one person lacked food, everyone knew. If they had a poor farm harvest compared to others, it became public information, open to analysis on whether laziness or wickedness had caused the farmer his misfortune. Secrets in that part of the world flew as quickly as the dusty breeze in the Sahara Desert, and hiding them was as difficult as having a snowball fight in hell.

UD had her personal business open for discussion all over the place, but she didn't care. Many parents warned their daughters to avoid her company and their sons to steer clear or she would make them father a pregnancy that wasn't theirs. She was nothing like her older sister, Akpana, who'd graduated from the university a few years ago and maintained a good level of discipline to everyone's admiration. Akpana was never seen on street corners with lousy company, and she dressed decently, especially for a child who had once lived with students from a variety of backgrounds in the university. As for Gregory, he may not have been a wealthy man, but he would support any child willing to 'bend down' and read, be it male or female. Gone were the days when people used to say, "Book na wor-wor food for woman pikin." Now, education was a very delicious delicacy for anybody who was ready to learn. So, yes, his children would be educated if they were willing, but nobody would waste his money on anything they had no interest in, so he'd left the choice open.

Breaking News

As 25th December drew nearer, Felicia and Ikel ensured all their kids had new sets of clothes and shoes ready, except for the older children, who claimed they were too old for Christmas clothes and shoes. The girls made fancy hairstyles days before, and the boys had clean haircuts with a side slit, a style Gregory only permitted on special occasions.

The women also bought food and special spices to give the day's meal a distinct taste and flavour from the usual. A big bag of Uncle Ben's rice was bought to make fluffy jollof rice. Usually, they used local rice, which had a lot of stones and dirt and required excessive washing and de-stoning. However, Uncle Ben's rice, although more expensive, had little to no stones and made special appearances for guests and family on special occasions.

Notwithstanding his financial struggles, all the money spent for the preparation came directly from the pocket of the man of the house: Gregory. The same financial situation that had sent him packing from Lagos had not only caught up with him in the village but had multiplied. In addition to emerging bills, he had been re-paying the loan he'd collected from the Bebuagbong community in Lagos from the proceeds of his farm, plus the pressure of caring for two wives, young children, and the older kids, who were moving up to higher education, all compounding the family bills.

He thought his first daughter, Akpana, would step in to provide for the family especially her younger siblings. After all, that was the advantage of having so many children. With time, the older ones began to care for the family, relieving their ageing parents from the financial stress.

But this expectation was unrealistic. Akpana, who had finished her university programme with distinction in Computer Science, was still struggling to get a decent job.

Gaining employment after her National Youth Service Corps (NYSC) programme proved challenging. The NYSC was a one-year compulsory national programme for all university graduates in Nigeria to serve their country. Akpana had made different job applications, but she kept receiving rejections and the unfortunately-on-this-occasion recruiter default email responses.

At last, she settled on being a private IT educator, teaching younger children how to use the computer. Due to the lack of government jobs across the country, most young people settled as primary school teachers in growing communities when they couldn't get a job.

While Akpana was at home for the Christmas break, her family's expectations were reflected in the signs and behaviours they gave her. For example, her mother complained out loud that she needed money to wash her waxy ears because she didn't want to go deaf and never hear the lovely Mass of Father Paul at Saint Theresa, the Little Flower Catholic Church. Her father, Gregory, sometimes refused to speak to her, and when he did, he spoke and responded through his nostrils. It was the same attitude they had displayed over the phone while she was in the city trying to make ends meet, but it was straight to her face this time. She remembered that a few times, she was tipped by kind parents as compensation for her hard work. All of that money was immediately sent to her parents, who called on the phone to praise her for being a good child and remembering them. They prayed immensely and encouraged her not to be weary of her generosity, but when Akpana didn't have enough, she expected some understanding, which she never received. Sometimes, Gregory reported to relatives how he had suffered to sponsor his first child up to university only for Akpana to turn her back on her family when they needed her the most. These comments and attitudes caused the young lady a lot of grief. If she were one of those desperate city girls, she might sell her soul to make her family as happy as they were whenever they 'heard' from her.

Luckily, one of her pupil's parents had connected her to a job opportunity abroad that would undoubtedly change her life, and she planned to tell her family about it that holiday.

On a cool evening, members of the Gregory family sat in their backyard to have their dinner. The cold Harmattan air was bearable that evening, so Gregory asked that they wear the comfortable sweaters and stockings Felicia had purchased from town with long trousers and wrappers to cover their legs from the cold and mosquitoes.

Whilst they waited for their food, the firewood stove used to prepare the family dinner was left lit and was fanned occasionally to keep everybody warm.

Felicia and her co-wife had successfully made a pot of soup without any fighting or quarrelling, and their husband was pleased about it. The preparation for the birth of Jesus Christ must have brought some peace to his family, he presumed, as he watched his kids serve large bowls of fufu with garnished beniseed soup.

The parents sat on high chairs and ate from the same bowls while the children formed clusters on a spread-out raffia mat and ate noisily, licking their fingers, smacking their lips, and gobbling up balls of fufu.

"Who pounded this fufu?" Gregory asked, rolling a lump in his hand.

Little Amokeye raised a finger. "It is me."

"Wonderful! You mean you pounded this lumpless fufu?"

"Yes, I did. Sister Akpana taught me how to pound it."

"And how old are you again?" Gregory asked, swallowing a big lump of fufu that bulged in his oesophagus like a car driving over a speed bump He relished the taste of the beniseed soup, licking his fingers and savouring the moment with his eyes half shut.

"I will be eleven years old next month," Amokeye replied.

"Wonderful! These daughters of mine are really making me proud," Gregory said.

"So, our little Amokeye is no longer so little. Just look at her smooth, lumpless fufu. Felicia and Ikel, can both of you put together pound fufu as good as this?" Ikel chuckled with her head bowed to the bowl of soup.

"Atiam Akpana, we will finish this food while you keep talking, o," Felicia advised.

"Allow me to praise my daughter, Felicia. The food can wait," Gregory cautioned. He continued, "Very soon, husbands will be trooping into my compound one after the other to ask for my daughters' hands in marriage, starting from my first daughter, Akpana—is it not so, Akpana?"

The spotlight fell on Akpana, with all eyes swaying in her direction.

"I have some news," Akpana said, breaking the brief silence.

"Ehen? You have a suitor?" her mother asked.

Akpana chuckled lightly. "Not a suitor, Ma, but I plan to travel overseas."

"Over what?" Felicia asked anxiously.

"Overseas, Ma. A company in England is sponsoring me on a five-year work visa if I can cover my travel cost and stay."

"Wonderful!" Gregory exclaimed, still in disbelief.

The family had paused eating as eyes widened in shock. Some balls of fufu dropped back in their plates. Others hurriedly gulped theirs in seconds while the rest continued to massage their fufu endlessly. The pin-drop silence was loud as the shocking revelation lingered in the air.

Travelling abroad was usually a huge milestone for many struggling families in Nigeria. It was an experience and opportunity usually reserved for the rich and elite classes. So, Akpana's breaking of the news sounded like a fairy tale and an unrealistic bargain.

"Do you mean England like the Queen's country?" Felicia asked, breaking the silence.

"Yes, Ma," Akpana replied.

With hazy thoughts about the news, Felicia stood up unsteadily and adjusted the loose wrapper around her waist. She quickly washed her hands in the small washbasin and waved them in the air.

"So, you mean me, Felicia, will soon be driving big-big cars, wearing expensive Hollandis wrappers when I go for our monthly meetings, and they will be calling me 'Mama London'?"

Felicia burst into a song, gyrating her hips and covering her left eye with her palm:

"Pepper them, Felicia, pepper them o,
Pepper them, Felicia, pepper them o,
Pepper them, Felicia, pepper them o."

"Felicia! That's enough of the peppering of imaginary enemies. Now, sit your buttocks down and let our daughter finish her speech," Gregory cautioned angrily. If looks could kill, Felicia would have fallen flat on the cold floor from Gregory's dagger-filled stare. She adjusted her wrapper aggressively and returned to her seat.

Amused by events, Ikel chuckled quietly. It was all she did lately. The girls had grown some horns and spoke back to her occasionally, especially in defence of their mother, so she picked her battles wisely and only poked at her senior wife when her older daughters were out of sight.

"Ehen, my dear, tell us more: what does this process entail, and who are these sponsors you speak of?" Gregory asked.

"It's a health care company. Apparently, there is a shortage of healthcare assistants in England, so the company is hiring overseas workers to care for their elderly service users."

"Is it not that job that they clean people's *nyash* (bums)? So, you want to go and pack *oyibo* (white people) shit and live as a second-class citizen in a foreign land? God forbid!" Ikel snapped two fingers over her head and buried her head in the bowl of soup again.

"Look at who is talking about being a second class in another man's home," Felicia said, visibly upset at Ikel's remarks. "Of all contributions to make, you thought yourself qualified to say what you just vomited? You better keep your envy to yourself and focus on your fufu before I —"

"Enough, Felicia! I said, enough! Just when I was praising God that there was no fighting this evening, you disappointed my thanksgiving with your drama. *Haba!* Any more interruptions from you or anyone else before this child finishes her speech will have disastrous consequences," Gregory warned.

Turning to Akpana, he said, "Look, my dear, whether it is domestic duties or packing faeces and cleaning butts, it doesn't matter. All I know is that they will pay you well for it, you hear me? So don't listen to your young mummy. You'll do well; I trust you," her father encouraged.

"Thanks, sir. I am aware of the nature of the job, and that is not an issue for me. I look after Ama Agnes when she falls ill, and it's the same skills required for the job."

"Good talk, my dear," Gregory said, "but is the sponsorship for free?"

"It's not free, per se, the employers are paying for it. They get the funds from the government to sponsor skilled workers."

"Oh, that is great. It makes life easier, then."

"Yes, but that's not all. There are other costs I will have to shoulder on my own, too. First, I'll need an international passport, and then I will need to do a health check at IOM (International Organisation for Migration) health assessment centre in Abuja. I will also have to bear the cost of the visa application, make all the travel arrangements, including flight tickets, and have some money to organise myself for at least three months after arrival, so it is not cheap."

"Wonderful!" Gregory said. "That is a lot of cost to bear and a lot of money to pay back. So, who will sponsor your flight ticket, accommodation, feeding and all those you have mentioned?

"That is where I need some support, sir. The little I saved from my teaching job will not be enough to cover all the expenses, so I would appreciate some family support to make this dream come true. A win for one is a win for all, and once I start working in the UK, I shall reimburse the family."

"Wonderful!" Gregory said, trying to figure out which bank he would rob to provide the required assistance.

"Sister Akpana, will you take me with you to London?" Lipeunim asked eagerly.

"Don't forget us when you reach there o, Madam London," UD remarked playfully.

"How long will you stay there?" Beyin asked, looking worried and missing her sister already.

"Sister Akpana, which bus will you use to London?" asked Utsu.

The family burst out laughing.

"She could as well use a *keke napep* (auto rickshaw). Silly question," Beyin said, still laughing.

"All I know is that I will be the only one in this house who will not cry when sister Akpana leaves," Atimanu challenged.

"Oh, please. You said that before we left Lagos and then cried a river on our departure day. Yen, yen, yen," Adeshi mocked.

"Let's bet." Atimanu stuck out her palm for Adeshi to tap it aggressively as a sign of a bet.

"Sister Akpana, who will buy me cheese balls and puff-puff when you travel?" Unimke asked tearily.

More questions and comments continued to pour out, though Akpana never had the chance to answer any of them as they kept talking over each other.

The rest of the evening meal dragged on too long. Though the parents were ecstatic about the possibility of their daughter travelling overseas, the financial burden was scary and daunting.

Although Gregory's farming business was doing well and the cost of living in the rural area was generally cheaper than in Lagos. However, he was still not financially buoyant enough to absorb the bills associated with his daughter's travel together with Lagos loan repayment with interest, the many mouths to feed and the school fees to pay had caused him a lot of financial strain.

Oh, if only he had been contented with his pay at the NRC and hadn't engaged in any 'backyard business', he would have been receiving his pension and gratuity by now, Gregory thought solemnly. There was a deep feeling of guilt in his heart. For once, he wondered what his family thought about him and what precedent he had set for his children to be responsible, non-scheming members of society.

Despite their financial woes, one must help a family to pave the way for other members of the same clan to progress. So what if he sold his small piece of land by the roadside to help Akpana move abroad?

Stainless-Bobo

"Stainless-Bobo!" The village kids hailed Ubi, who was neatly dressed in white from head to toe.

"*Whatsup*, my people?" he replied with a smile, wiping the Harmattan dust with his white handkerchief as he bounced about the village in a pair of 'I-swear-to-God' shoes that pointed to the sky.

Despite the dusty Harmattan season, Ubi maintained the impeccable style of dressing that had earned him the name 'Stainless'.

Everyone knew the man, Stainless, as an American returnee, who was now one of the three 'been-tos' in the village. He was an excellent entertainer who thrilled his audiences, especially the kids, with his foreign accent and poetic grammar. From his cheerful look, one might guess that America had been good to him. He occasionally entertained questions about the country and regularly demonstrated

America's way of life while chattering with a funny accent, which was quite different from the ones they heard in the movies. "I wanna get a boddle of wadder from the shop," Stainless said, sounding American. That made the kids laugh hard.

"Stainless-Bobo, you will not kill us with this, your big-big oyibo grammar. Is it bottled water that you are calling boddle wadder?" the kids replied, laughing.

"Was it not just yesterday that Ubi travelled overseas? And here he is, blowing big-big grammar and speaking through his nose with the white man's accent like he was born there," Kene said to his friend, James. They were regular customers at Adaku's Palm Wine and Pepper Soup joint, chatting, drinking and betting on games.

James belched loudly and pointed his finger in the air as if he could see an invisible figure standing there. "I heard he was deported from America." His speech slurred from drinking too much palm wine.

"Olololoo! No wonder he came back with nothing. Penniless. Just moving about with an American accent in his mouth. Can accent pay bills?" Kene asked, staggering with a calabash of palm wine under his armpit. "Madam Adaku, more palm wine!" he called out.

Although Stainless was a been-to like others, he was not as forthcoming with money as the rest. The people had an assumption that anyone who had been abroad or lived there was wealthy. They expected that upon arrival, an entourage escorted the returnee from the airport with a fanfare that created an atmosphere of extravaganza, including a fleet of cars and the spraying of minted notes as the returnee made their way home, just like in many Nollywood Movies. Unfortunately, it doesn't end with the expected flamboyant arrival. A lot of visitors came from far and near, each person with a set of expectations and problems to be solved. Realistically, this was the situation with some immigrants from developing communities and one of the reasons they engaged themselves in extra work to meet community expectations.

Many immigrants indulged these expectations by working late-night shifts and doing a lot of overtime jobs before travelling back home to keep up with the financial expectations of their status as a 'been-to', fostering the narrative about people who travelled abroad for greener pastures.

Surprisingly, this was not the case for Stainless. He was an '*aka superglue*' (tight-fisted), and to compensate for his inability to show some 'love' to the people, he used big grammar and an American accent to feign ignorance of the expected.

Nobody knew Stainless's aim for returning to his maternal village after five years of being away. Since it was the end of the year, when many people visited home, Ubi was home like everyone else.

"Stainless-Bobo! When we go see, knor?" James called Stainless from a distance with a strong Bette accent as if he genuinely cared to have a meet and greet with him. If they met at all, he would tax Stainless to buy him more palm wine and pepper soup. Stainless knew these antics and simply replied with wisdom: "At the parry tonight, dawg! See you there, my brother."

Soon, it was evening, and the atmosphere became jubilant with the party mood setting in. As was the custom with the 'been-tos', Stainless had arrived at the party on time with a clean, white, buttoned short-sleeved shirt and white jean shorts. He sat with his legs crossed, showcasing a white palm slipper.

The atmosphere that night was euphoric. Underneath the twinkling stars in the chilly Harmattan evening were young men and women from neighbouring communities—Bebuatsuan, Kakum, Ukambi, Igwo, Bebuaabie and many others—all gathered to celebrate the annual Christmas Eve event. Bebuagbong village hosted the other villages and made a show of it in an attempt to beat the previous hosts of the event in a silent competition.

In the front row sat a few elderly people in special reclining bamboo seats. They were all well-dressed in sweaters, long trousers and wrappers that kept them warm as they chatted over cups of palm wine, garden eggs and kola nuts.

The young and more agile ones viewed the scene standing at a distance. Some stood on stools while others stretched their necks for a clearer view. A few latecomers hung onto tree branches like the biblical Zacchaeus, stretching to see Jesus from a sycamore tree. There was a firm reliance on the moon to shine its light on the night's activities, and nature's gift did not disappoint. The moon shone its brightest, peeking through the colossal mango tree under which the event had occurred.

The first group to showcase what they had been working on was the boys to men Age Grade, a group of boys aged thirteen to seventeen years. Theirs was a traditional dance display with costumes of raffia palm fibre covering their bodies. The young boys became unrecognisable once they put on their face masks. At that moment, they ceased to be the sons, grandsons, brothers or nephews everyone knew; they became revered masquerades, embodying the spirits of the living and the dead. During the day, the masqueraders chased people around the village community to create some fun. In other cultures, the masqueraders chased people with long wooden canes. Woe betides anyone caught in the chase; such a person would be thoroughly flogged or need some money to be bailed out for their freedom but the Obudu masqueraders were usually nicer, and at night, they were sweet entertainers, dancing in the moonlight and thrilling their audiences. The fun was the suspense created in the ushering in of the masqueraders into the playground. No one knew exactly where the masqueraders would pop out from.

Suddenly, the people felt a massive force springing from the path leading to the nearby valley towards the event scene, chanting the tribal *Bette* eulogy:

"Kugbudu—blayebe (People of Obudu—aren't we the one's)?"

And the crowd responded—"Bla(We are)!"

"Blayebe (Aren't we the ones)?" They asked again.

"Bla (We are)!" came a louder response from the crowd.

As they approached the gathering spectators, a cheer went out from the crowd. People stretched their necks like ostriches to get a full view from their corners. Some even tried to guess who might be wearing which costume. The drummers hit the drums between their legs as if it were no man's business, and the crowd clapped and cheered endlessly until the display ended.

Next, the cultural dancers moved in to temper the heightened mood after the intensity of the masquerade display. UD led the group, singing and dancing rhythmically to the beat of the drums. When it came to beauty and talent, every discerning person around saw it in Udanshi Ipeh. Her voice was as smooth as butter, and the twisting of her waist was like that of an earthworm. She moved her chubby feet to the beat of the drums, never skipping a beat as she sang her heart out, displaying her gap tooth. Her melanised skin refused to blend in with the dark sky, shining like a ray of sunlight piercing through the night. All eyes were on her, and she not only knew how to shine but also how to retain the centre light on herself.

Meanwhile, Stainless sat in a corner, watching each event as they unfolded. He watched UD's performance in awe, gasping in wonder at the uniqueness of the rare beauty before him and wondered if she could be the one.

"*Mashi akie eeeh! Mashi akie*! (Well done to you all!)," voices screamed from the crowd as the cultural dancers wrapped up their performance. There was clapping and whistling, with the older women ululating. Most of these women reminisced about the good old days. A few things had changed here and there, but the dance was still a joy to watch. There was no need to compare the good old days to the present; change was constant.

Stainless seized the opportunity to follow the lead singer and dancer, a girl who, at a glance, may have captured his heart.

"Excuse me…excuse me." Stainless squashed his way through the jam-packed crowd. "Sorry, Ama. Sorry, everyone. Please, let me squeeze through, thank you. My apologies, Apa, thank you."

There was a lot of squabbling to accommodate Stainless's annoying movement as he wriggled tenaciously through the crowd.

"Hello, beauty—may I have a minute?" Stainless asked UD, who was gobbling a cup of water to quench her thirst after her rigorous singing and dancing.

She kept silent until she had finished the last drop of water in the cup. "What for?" she asked coldly.

"Come on, beauty. I just want to be your friend."

"I'm cool, boo. I do not need new friends."

Stainless was taken aback. A pretty girl with a hostile demeanour—what a mismatch! UD, on the other hand, was simply playing by the unspoken rule of a boy-girl relationship, which was to show barely any interest upon first approach or risk appearing cheap and desperate. Besides, playing a little hard to get never hurt anyone, and if he really wanted her, he would prove himself worthy by persistently pursuing her, given the value of her worth.

"I saw you dancing with the other ladies, but your beauty stood out for me. The way you moved your feet to the rhythm of the drums was as effortless as the sea waves wriggling that magnificent waist of yours like a salted earthworm. Even your hips do not lie; perhaps you are related in some way to Shakira?"

UD giggled softly—her small lips tightly pressed together, revealing two dimples on her cheeks. Stainless had hit a soft spot. Imagine being compared to the famous Shakira. *Haaa*! She must have hit the jackpot, but the young man must not know she was beginning to like him, so she chinned up and adjusted her blouse in a lackadaisical manner. Her shiny brown eyes still seemed to give her innermost desire away with their sudden glow.

Stainless broke the brief silence. "So…may I at least know your name?"

"You seem to be very pushy," UD said.

"Well, what can a man do? Your beauty has me wrapped up like a newborn in the arms of its mother. So, you care to tell me your name?"

"May I know yours first, Mr. Lover Boy?"

"Oh, my apologies. My name is Ubi, but everyone calls me Stainless."

"Oh, you are the Stainless-Bobo I hear about. I should have guessed, with your white-on-white appearance despite the dusty Harmattan wind flying around."

"Funny you." Stainless smiled shyly.

"My name is Udanshi, but my friends call me UD."

"Oh, wow! UD—what a lovely name for a rare gem. Stainless-Bobo X UD—how classic. Could I also have your phone number, if you don't mind? I'd like us to talk more to know each other better."

"Oh! Trouble has found me today. You seem to be pushing your luck, young man. I just gave you my name;

now you need my phone number? Who knows your next request—my home address?"

"Pardon me, *mademoiselle*. I'm no trouble at all. Do me this last favour, and you'll make my Christmas a happy one."

UD smiled at the French insertion. Stainless seemed to be doing everything right, and for a moment, she forgot she had Bambeshi, who she had just started a relationship with, but there she was, falling in love with a stranger. She would go ahead with it to see where it led, she thought. Besides, a fellow once said, "When the desirable is not available, the available becomes the desirable," And this available chap was quickly becoming desirable to her.

"Do you see that lass sitting under that mango tree over there?" UD spoke, pointing towards the tree.

"Yes, I do."

"She's my younger sister, Beyin. Tell her I sent you, and she'll give you my phone number. Bye, Mr. Lover Boy." She walked off, leaving Stainless desperately curious about the belle's mysterious personality. One minute, she seemed cold and unwavering; another minute, she was considerate while maintaining her rigidity.

Many days had passed since UD and Stainless met. The duo became inseparable talking late into the night with the MTN 'extra cool' package, which allowed callers to call fellow MTN service users for free from midnight to dawn.

They talked about anything and everything as butterflies rumbled in their tummies.

UD clung to her phone as if her life depended on it, grinning from ear to ear whenever the phone rang. Sometimes, she moved aimlessly to different parts of the house while on the phone with her lover, scratching the wall, mumbling inaudible words and giggling softly. She would go to America with Stainless, the love of her life, whose sparkling eyes lit up her gloominess and whose gentle whispers melted her heart.

"Will you marry me?" Stainless asked one fine evening, with one knee on the floor. He organised a pleasant engagement dinner in one of the happening places in town, and UD screamed joyfully, "Yes! Yes! I will," sticking out the middle finger on her left hand.

Stainless's joy knew no bounds. He had fulfilled his quest, the reason for returning to the village after five years of being away.

With the urgency of his needing to return to where he was based, a marriage had to be done. Although they had only known each other for a couple of months, it felt like forever. UD couldn't wait any longer to experience the life her lover had painted in her mind about the ease of life in America, the land of the free and the home of the brave. She would marry this man and never have any trouble in her life. She told him of her dreams of becoming a reality TV star, and Stainless was thrilled. He called her an industrious woman who had goals that must be nurtured. She'd hit the jackpot with such a man. Not even her father would consent to such ideas from any of his beloved wives.

The Traditional Marriage

The village women danced around the Ipeh family compound. They swung their hips from side to side as if to tell the people these oldies still had it. It was the marriage ceremony of Stainless and his pearl, UD.

Weeks before, Stainless and his uncle had visited the Ipehs. His uncle had said to Gregory after they had been offered a seat, "My name is Bassey, and this is my nephew, Ubi. He invited me all the way from Ugep in Yakuur to come to Obudu and see you for something very important."

Gregory had adjusted himself properly. He knew that whatever they had to say was very important. "Okay, I'm all ears," Gregory had said.

"Thank you, sir," Bassey had said. He continued, "Like people always say, if you see a toad running in the daytime, it's either it's chasing something or something is chasing it."

"Mmmmh….that is correct," Gregory had said.

"We have seen a beautiful flower in your garden and thought it wise to seek your permission to pluck it, sir," Bassey had said.

"You have spoken well, my wonderful guest. If I may ask, which of the flowers in my garden do you seek?"

Stainless had beamed with a smile. "UD, sir."

"Wonderful!" Gregory had exclaimed, smiling from ear to ear.

"It's all right. I hear you, and I appreciate your visit," Gregory had said. "However, as you may already know, in our culture, marriage is not only between a man and a woman but between their families as well, so you people will have to come again when my relatives would be around to bear witness to what I have heard you say today."

The Bette people had a unique marriage culture where a man attended several visits to his prospective in-laws along with performing certain marital rites before he married the lady he wished to marry. Stainless had known all of this and made sure he ticked all the boxes. He and members of his immediate family had visited for the second time with kegs of palm wine and kola nuts, wrappers, and travelling boxes, a bottle of schnapps and bush meat along with other souvenirs to greet the family as a part of the requirements for the marital rites.

Stainless had also paid a bride price to his father-in-law. Gregory had received the envelope with gratitude, tore it open, took a thousand naira note from the bulk of the money and returned the rest to Stainless.

"I appreciate your kind gesture, my son, but my precious daughter, UD, is not for any price, so I give you back the bulk of your money. However, this one thousand naira note that I have taken is a sign that I accept you as my son-in-law, and I give you my daughter's hand in marriage with joy and an open heart."

After all the in-house sorting and consultations, the big day had come. Friends and family from all walks of life assembled to celebrate with the lovebirds.

They sat under various canopies, shielding themselves from the blazing sun that rose to the occasion. Above the canopies were cardboard papers with names written on them to distinguish where the audience members were to sit. One of the canopies was decorated for the couple, another for the bride and groom's family, and others for visiting guests and extended family members. The people waited patiently for the bride, who had been indoors with her maidens, putting herself together to dazzle her groom. They entertained themselves with some good music and fresh palm wine while chatting and exchanging pleasantries, especially between family members who had not seen each other for a long time. Soon, the MC announced that the bride would soon be out, which increased their anticipation.

With the sound of ululations and joyful cheer, the bride stepped out of her chamber with an air of confidence and grace. Her beauty was as radiating as the sun, with an artistic makeover that enriched her appearance. Her braided hair tied down to the back of her head was embellished with cowries, which were an indication of affluence.

She was well put-together, and the elegance she exuded captivated the hearts of her guests, who twisted their necks in her direction.

As it was her big day, she shone brightly in an embellished purple George fabric. Felicia feared that one of the guests might wear a design similar to that of the bride and ruin her big moment, so she had travelled many miles with UD to acquire sophisticated and unique fabrics from Abuja. A piece of the fabric was tied around UD's waist, and its end was tucked back into the wrapper to keep it firm. The wrapper was short enough to arouse curiosity but long enough to cover the subject matter as it hugged her figure, revealing her curves and chunky thighs down to her feet. Around her chest was a second wrapper that matched and exposed a bit of her cleavage in a bid to show what her 'mama gave her'.

Her neck was not left bare: two large red coral beads hung over her bosom, complimenting her attire, with another set of tiny red beads that swung around her waist as she wriggled to the tune of the music. Even the earth agreed with her tempo as it absorbed the sweat dripping from her thick thighs that were heated from rubbing against each other.

The groom, Stainless, had invited a live musical band to add vibrance to the occasion. As soon as they saw the bride stepping out, they began singing the artist Flavour N'abania's famous song, "Ada-Ada": A song that talked about a beautiful lady that looked as fresh as tomatoes who would be pregnant with a boy and girl child exactly nine months after her marriage. It was the song of the moment. With skilful purpose, UD bent her waist low with her bum popping out behind her. She nodded her head in the style of an agama lizard, with her arms spread out like a proud peacock showcasing its beauty.

Lifting one foot in the air, she twirled from side to side and then up and down, her smiles decorating her dance steps with an aura of tranquillity, and the village women ululated in solidarity with the skilful movement.

She waved at her guests with a horsetail that signified royalty. Even though she had no royal heritage, she was allowed to feel like a royal, just this once in her lifetime.

"She looks so robust," one observer whispered in admiration. "She must be living well," said another. Similar comments echoed through the crowd, made mostly by the male guests.

Many years ago, especially amongst the Efik people of Southern-Nigeria, it was a cultural practice for men to marry plump women. Some women had to go through a fattening process to achieve that standard of beauty to look 'appealing' to their prospective husbands and in-laws. This paragon of allurement still lingers in some Nigerian tribes.

The young maidens were also nicely dressed up for the big day. They danced behind the bride in admiration with wishful thoughts. Some rolled their eyes enviously, trying hard to find fault with the bride's hair and makeup. A few maidens came with the intent of grabbing a suitor. They pretended to dance while their eyes scanned about, checking for admirers. As soon as a manly figure looked their way, their tempo increased, and they moved their backsides violently like bouncing balls. Observers would argue that these ladies where 'desparados' on duty.

Felicia tied a big blue gele headwrap on her head to match her silver lace blouse and blue George wrapper. She stood up occasionally, pretending to adjust the big wrapper tied around her waist just to be noticed by all the other women in case they forgot who the mother of the day was. Before she'd had her only son, Unimke, it was these same women who'd mocked her delivery of female children, but now who was laughing? One of her daughters was getting married on that day to a man from America who had a lot of money. Imagine the kind of money that would begin to roll in when the couple had settled abroad.

Felicia's joy knew no bounds as she watched her daughter in the glory of her elegance. She felt proud of herself for raising such a gem and bragged out loud to the other women who were seated under the red canopy designated for the family: "Just take a look at my daughter, UD, a well-kept and discipline child. Which man wouldn't pride himself in marrying such a lady, eh?"

"You did well, my sister," one woman exclaimed, giving Felicia two thumbs up.

"It is difficult to raise disciplined children in this day and time, you did well with yours," another woman concurred.

Ikel eyed her co-wife as she spoke, pouting her lips in her direction and turned stylishly to the side with her hand supporting her jaw to show that Felicia was telling an awful amount of lies. Who would say that their mother's pot of soup was not sweet? This was the same Felicia, who had fought some of her daughters, especially that one with a coconut head that went by the name of UD. She danced to the beat of her own drums, and good counsel, to her, was a story for the gods. Their rushed marriage was evidence that she was probably digging for gold, or maybe she was already pregnant—who knew? Now, Felicia boasted of her sainthood, feigning ignorance of the obvious truth.

Meanwhile, UD danced, making her way to her father and his kinsmen to receive a cup of palm wine.

She had specifically requested to do a wine carrying to her husband. This was not the typical Bette cultural practice. However, many people tapped into other cultures in Nigeria through their dress style and cultural obligations.

Besides, UD was marrying a foreigner, and her family obliged to her request of infusing different cultural practices on her special day.

"Udanshi Ipeh, our beloved daughter, take this palm wine to the man you have agreed to marry. Let him drink from it to show that both of you are in agreement regarding this union," Ukandi Emma, the oldest sibling of the Ipeh family, said to UD, who knelt before him as a sign of respect.

UD received the drink and supported it with her free hand to prevent spillage. She stood up with the help of her maidens and danced around gracefully in search of her groom. Some young men stretched their hands to receive the palm wine from the new bride, even men old enough to be UD's grandpa. These gestures created a lot of fun in traditional marriage ceremonies, leaving non-participants laughing their lungs out and some women getting upset at their significant others for daring to stretch out their palms, too. The whisperers said that if the bride handed the cup of palm wine to any of the men and they drank from it, they automatically became the husband of the new bride, but no one in history had ever played such games for the whispers to be confirmed.

A village man hailed Stainless, who was hiding out of sight to make his new bride search longer for him just for the fun of it. "My guy, na man, you be." The admirer wished he had approached the bride before Stainless did, but it was too late now. All he could do was feed his eyes at the magnificence of the belle before them.

Stainless peeked from his hiding spot at his bride, who was desperately searching for him in the crowd. His eyes appeared dreamy, not believing his luck to have been accepted by this rare beauty. In those days, amongst the Bette people, many families arranged marriages for their children, so the couple barely knew each other before the day of their union. Many grew their love, while others endured their marriage till their dying days. What never changed was the bride price the groom's family paid to the bride's family in appreciation of the beauty they had maintained. Stainless thought of all this, and some form of manly pride beamed on his face. He stroked his own ego as he had met the requirements of marrying his bride traditionally, as a real man should.

Now, the scorching sun hit UD and her maidens—who had been dancing for half an hour. She needed to find her groom and end the search as she was parched.

Finally, she saw her man Ubi—Stainless—seated at the back of a yellow canopy in the distance, with his white-on-white lace kaftan and a purple cap to match his bride. "Fine man," she said to herself, admiring her husband. She presented the cup of palm wine to him, looking straight into his eyes as if to conjure some spells to make him fall harder in love with her. He drank, acknowledging that he was the chosen one. Everyone clapped, and the village women ululated louder this time.

Stainless and his bride danced their way to their parents, who blessed their union one family at a time. "May God bless your home, and may you be fruitful and multiply," they prayed, and a resounding, "Amen!" came from the crowd.

The couple went in to freshen up and returned to the occasion with matching outfits. UD was decently dressed in a short-sleeved silver lace top and gele. She tied a two-piece, purple George wrapper around her waist to her feet. This was a subtle way of announcing her new status as a responsible married woman. Her husband was dressed in a Niger-Delta white etibo and trousers with a felt hat and walking stick. He tied the same George wrapper as his wife around his waist and walked with style. Well-wishers sprung from their seats as if being stung by bees. They reached into their pockets and purses for minted notes and sprayed cash generously on the couple. Some Igbo men that lived and did business in Obudu spoke their language to hail the beautiful bride: "*Omalicha nwa* (beautiful one), *tomato jos* (fresh tomatoes), a*sampete* (beautiful lady)." The village women rolled their tongues, ululating from time to time. Even the children joined in, singing and dancing joyfully with their mouths stuffed with jollof rice. The village drunks, James and Kene, whose favourite outings were occasions such as that, drank palm wine to a stupor and opened their mouths wide, cursing everybody as they revealed secrets only known to drunks.

As for the couple, they had found each other, and what God had joined together, let no man put asunder.

Giant Step

UD and Stainless's marriage being the talk of the town was over. The couple was enjoying their honeymoon at the Obudu Cattle Ranch, a delectable destination for such an occasion. It was quiet, serene and away from the hustling and bustling atmosphere of the township.

Now, the entire Ipeh family had all the time to focus on Akpana, whose travel visa to England had been granted.

Felicia danced and danced around the family house as her girls were making her proud. A few weeks ago, UD and her husband had done a traditional marriage that had gathered their friends and foes to the grand celebration. Now, Akpana was travelling abroad to work. Haa! She was reaping the dividends of her children while she was still alive, thank God!

The family had a hushed party for their daughter, inviting only trusted family and friends to send her off. The fear of sharing the good news with people who might jinx the blessing was a thing most Nigerians dreaded. Many people only told their family and friends about their journey once abroad. Ultimately, they called to apologise from a foreign telephone number, leaving their once-healthy relationship sometimes scarred for life. However, they would rather destroy their relationships with people than ruin their travel opportunities with envious minds, sending out negative vibes. It was with this in mind that the Ipeh family kept Akpana's send-off party a secret.

As penance for the discomfort Gregory had caused his family through his misconduct at his well-paid job in Lagos, he tried to make up for it by throwing his total weight into whatever would make life worthwhile for his family. He supported Akpana with a massive sum of money from his sold piece of land and parted with some money he had saved for a rainy day. The funds would help Akpana pay for her flight ticket, get a good apartment, and settle some bills for the first few months after arriving in England.

Felicia did not sit as a spectator to her child's start in a foreign land. She bought many African food items,—*egusi*, crayfish, beniseed, groundnut, dried fish and stock fish, seasoning cubes, palm oil and other food items. Atimanu and Beyin helped peel the egusi, blew the shaft out, and blended them nicely for Akpana to make her favourite soup whenever she wanted. The groundnuts were also fried and blended for stews and soups. The basket of crayfish was cleaned up and blended, too. The whole family came through to support their own.

Akpana appreciated her family's efforts, especially those of her father, who had to sell his piece of land for her sake. Soon, she would be in England, but she would never forget her family's sacrifices.

****

Gregory had escorted his daughter to Abuja, where they spent the night in a paid guesthouse prior to Akpana's departure day. Both father and daughter arrived at the Nnamdi Azikiwe International Airport the next day, pulling bags of luggage containing many African food items and essentials to make the first few months in England easier.

Soon, it was time for Akpana to check in her luggage, and both father and daughter had to say their final goodbyes. Akpana embraced her father as she watched him shed a few tears. "Don't worry, apa. I will be all right," she told him.

"Be a good girl for me, and always remember the family you come from," Gregory said.

Akpana nodded her head and wiped a few tears away, too. "Goodbye, apa," she said in a croaky voice with a lump in her throat.

"Represent us well, my daughter," Gregory said to her with a final hug.

"I love you, apa," she said to her father, but as was typical of many Nigerian fathers his age, Gregory said an awkward OK, so she went off into the sterile area of the airport with mixed emotions, excited to go into the big bird with gigantic wings that would fly for hours in the air and sad to miss her family too.

With the excitement of her first flight experience, Akpana located her seat by the window and placed her hand luggage in an open compartment above her head.

It wasn't too long before a voice spoke: "Good evening, ladies and gentlemen. My name is Captain Kadijat Ahmed, and I welcome everyone on board the Qatar Airways flight leaving the Nnamdi Azikiwe Airport in Abuja to Dubai International Airport. The local time is 10.30 p.m., and we hope to arrive at about 5 a.m. If you need any assistance, please feel free to speak to the cabin crew. Thank you for flying with us. Sit back and enjoy your flight."

Akpana listened attentively. The speaker's Arabic accent was foreign to her Nigerian ears. She didn't hear everything the soothing voice said, especially about the plane's altitude and some of the other terminology the captain used.

Soon, a slender white lady with a radiating smile walked up to the front of the plane. She held a manual in her hand and talked about safety procedures. Another flight attendant stood by her, wearing a bright red lipstick that shone like a mirror from a distance, she demonstrated the use of the equipment being talked about. Akpana struggled again with the accent, but she watched the demonstrations carefully and copied a few things, like fastening her seatbelt, while grasping the concept of an emergency evacuation.

The flight experience was nerve-racking yet thrilling. She looked from her window seat, watching with fascination as the plane moved on the runway at a succession of slow to breakneck speed. When the plane was suspended in the air, her heart skipped, imagining all kinds of things that could go wrong.

Akpana continued to observe the interior of the big bird that conveyed them with its massive wings. At the back of the seat in front of her were some nice magazines tucked into a net pocket that cajoled her with their bright images and made her want to have a look. Above them was a mini food tray that fell flat to her face when she turned the knob on the tray clockwise. At the top of the mini food tray was a small screen with a variety of TV channels. She would explore the channels and pick a good movie to watch later, she thought happily.

The rest of the flight experience was memorable. For once, Akpana felt pampered like a queen, not having to look after her younger ones or the elderly members of her family as she used to do in Nigeria. Here, the cabin crew took care of her, serving her meals and asking if she needed anything else. She ate and relaxed, watched a few movies, and drifted soundly to sleep.

Many hours had passed, but they felt like minutes as she was wrapped up in a blanket while being served and entertained. Soon, there was another announcement: the flight had reached Dubai International. Akpana got ready with her hand luggage and waited for the right time to exit the plane.

Next was to find her connecting flight to Birmingham Airport. The young lady observed carefully. The fear of missing her next flight was crippling, so she asked the airport staff a lot of questions while reading sign boards and carefully listening to the foreign accents for a departure call for Birmingham.

It didn't take too long before Akpana heard the departure call that tallied with an electronic screen displaying her destination. She followed a queue and was thrilled for another ride on the big bird with large wings. The staff were just as nice, only this time, she knew what to do as everything was the same as on the previous flight.

After many hours on the flight, Akpana landed safely at the Birmingham Airport in the United Kingdom. There was an internal dancing and thanksgiving that went on in her grateful heart. Being the first member of her family to arrive in a country as great as England called for jubilation. She knew her mother would organise a thanksgiving mass the next Sunday to celebrate her great feat, dancing in her usual fashion and singing off-key to the annoyance of the choir.

The young lady mumbled a quick prayer and hopped excitedly to grab her luggage.

As soon as she came out of the plane, she looked around in admiration. England was a beauty to behold, just like the glimpse of Dubai she had managed to grab in her memory while hurrying to catch her connecting flight. The environment was crisp and clear, with fast-walking people who had smiles that faded quickly when you stared away from their direction. After a few questions, she was lucky to have met a young lady who helped her find the trains to Loughborough, where she had paid for a room before her arrival.

When the train arrived, she made her way to her new home in a black cab. The black cabs cost an arm and a leg, as their charges were pay-as-you-go. A bus would have been more economical, but mistakes like that were usual for new arrivals.

Greener Pastures

Akpana arrived in England during the winter season. The weather was chilly, with temperatures dropping rapidly. On some days, it rained like it was no man's business. Many people carried umbrellas, while others wore waterproof, hooded jackets.

The season's gloom caused a rapid movement from people, springing off with their hoodies half-covering their faces, their hands buried in their pockets. Despite the weather conditions, their daily needs had to be tended to. Akpana observed the melancholia from the comfort of her bedroom window. The good news was that the dark, depressing winter was a waiting period for better days. Like the rainfall before the sunshine, everyone anticipated the glorious spring season with brighter days and sprouting flowers. Best of all, there was the warmness of the summer season.

The Care Is Life Company manager, Mr Koffi, had scheduled a face-to-face training session for Akpana. It would be their first meeting since her arrival. The lass put a few things together and eagerly awaited her new start with the company that had made it possible for her to travel overseas through a work visa sponsorship.

"Hello, Akpana…did I get the pronunciation right?" asked Koffi.

"Yes, sir," Akpana responded.

"Great! Have you been to England before or is this your first time?" he asked.

"This is my first time, sir. I lived in Nigeria all through."

"Right, that is not a problem at all. You are welcome to England. I hope you are settling in nicely?"

"Yes, thank you, sir. I am familiarising myself with my new environment. Almost everything is different here, but I'm positive about the process," Akpana replied.

"That's great to know. You are welcome to Care Is Life. As discussed before your arrival, your duties are simple yet delicate. You will be responsible for looking after our elderly service users. They all have different needs and levels of attention. Some require personal assistance with the shower, toilet and dressing up. Others only require you to keep them company or make their meals. Whatever it is, you will be trained to carry out the job, especially how to conduct CPR and transfer service users from one point to another in a safe manner for you and them. I hope you understand your responsibilities."

"Yes, sir, I believe I do."

"Hmm, Akpana, I understand the culture as I also come from West Africa—Ghana, to be precise—but here in England, we call people by their first names, so just call me Koffi."

"Okay, sir. Sorry...Koffi," Akpana said, blushing.

Koffi laughed. "That's all right. It might take a while, but you'll get used to life here with time."

"I believe so. Thanks very much for your help, Koffi. I will work very hard and always do my best for the company," Akpana said.

"I'm happy to hear that. Your training begins today. Feel free to ask all the questions about anything you need to know."

"All right, Koffi. Thank you."

"No problem, Akpana. Please make your way to the right and acquaint yourself with your colleagues while you wait for your trainer to take over."

****

The job of being a health care assistant seemed like a breeze to Akpana. Wasn't it just looking after people, preparing their meals and keeping them company? She already did much of that, being the first daughter in a family of nine children. The few things she wasn't very familiar with were using a sling to transfer patients safely and how to do CPR, but the trainer had been kind enough to let her have multiple practices on the dummy during training.

Feeling fully equipped to do the job, she woke up at 5 a.m. to prepare to take a bus to her service users. She was to begin at Mr Clarkson's home at 6 a.m.

Akpana had to learn to use Google Maps to locate the bus stands, bus times, and bus routes. Since arriving in England, she had missed her bus a few times after getting the bus time wrong or standing at the wrong bus stop.

If you missed a bus by a few seconds, you had to wait for the next bus, even if it took another hour. However, this couldn't occur on her first day of work, for any delay would cause a crisis for the whole care team, so she mapped out her bus routes days before.

That lovely morning, she dressed up in her well-ironed work uniform, a sky-blue shirt with the "Care Is Life" (CIL) name and logo on her left breast pocket and paired it with plain black trousers. She picked up her navy-blue hooded jacket and dashed out to the bus stand. The bus stopped at different destinations, and passengers had to press a red button to alert the driver of their bus stop. This fascinated Akpana on her first day on the bus. In Lagos, the passengers had to scream at the top of their lungs, "*Owa o* (I have arrived)!" Even at that, some drivers still passed the bus stops of most passengers, which was one of the reasons for some of the driver and passenger fights in Lagos, but here, they used buttons and not their voices. She also observed that they thanked the driver while exiting the bus, which was another strange discovery—why should you thank a driver for doing his job? When the bus approached the City Centre in Loughborough, Akpana pressed the button just before her exact location, and the bus stopped to let a few people out at the bus stop. "Thank you! Thank you!" the passengers said as they exited the bus. Akpana joined the chorus, "Thank You!" and made her way out.

Loughborough is the second largest city after Leicester in the county of Leicestershire. It is a tranquil city with a large population of England's senior citizens. The Care Is Life company pitched its tent there, where it gathered a good number of service users.

Mr Clarkson, an aged widower whose only child lived abroad, was one of those Care Is Life service users. He was the first person Akpana attended to on that fine morning.

Akpana rang the doorbell and waited for a reply. When she was done with Mr Clarkson, she would walk a few minutes to Lady Janet's home and then another service user until five people had been catered to that morning. In all, she would work a twelve-hour shift four days a week and have three days of rest.

Akpana underestimated the English weather. On her first day at work, she wore an unpadded *okrika* (second-hand) jacket her mother had purchased from Abuja, with flat black shoes. There were no gloves, hat, or scarf to keep her warm. She had begun to shiver when she heard footsteps approaching the door.

"Good morning, sir," an excited Akpana greeted Mr Clarkson with a bright smile on her face.

Mr Clarkson replied grumpily, "Morning. It seems you are new."

"Yes, sir. I just began today."

"Come in. I hope you know what to do. I prefer old faces as they give less hassle."

"I will do my best with the information given to me, sir."

"And what's your name?"

"My name is Akpana, sir."

"A-pi-ni?"

"No, sir, A-kpa-na?"

"What does that mean?"

"Akpana is a loose pronunciation. The original Bette pronunciation is 'Kukpana', which means 'a precious jewel'."

"Precious! I think I can remember that better than A-kpi-na… Shall I call you Precious, then?"

"It's fine, sir."

"Clarkson, please. Just call me Clarkson."

"I'm sorry, si—Clarkson."

Clarkson was quiet. Had she said or done anything wrong? As for her name, maybe she should have insisted that Clarkson called her Akpana—it was not a difficult name to remember or pronounce if one was determined to get it right, after all she had just heard the name Clarkson for the first time and had learnt to pronounce it. She tried to be quieter during the care process and only spoke when she needed to for fear of saying the wrong things.

"I would like two poached eggs, a slice of toast and a cup of coffee for breakfast, please."

"Yes, Clarkson," Akpana replied and dashed into the kitchen, unsure of what to do. During the care training, an acquaintance had told her she would, undoubtedly, make a few mistakes on her first days until she got used to the activities. From the look of things, she was about to make her first mistake. What were poached eggs? Couldn't he have asked for boiled or fried eggs instead? If he wanted his eggs fried, she would have prepared it nicely with diced tomatoes and onions with fresh peppers and spiced it up with seasoning like her mother used to do, and he would have enjoyed eating his fried eggs between two slices of freshly baked bread if he had any, but no, the man was asking for poached eggs.

"Aha!" she said, and she grabbed her phone from her small cross bag and went on Google, her new digital oracle and best friend since arriving in England. For everything you didn't know in the UK, just google it, not excluding her buddy, Google Maps. "Oh!" She said, reading some articles and watching short YouTube videos, her mouth agape. It was simply cooking cracked eggs in boiling water for a few minutes with a lot of precision and good timing. She tried to imitate the video she'd watched and came up with a mockery of what poached eggs should be. The egg yolk ran to one side, and the egg white looked frail and way undercooked.

Clarkson smiled. "You will have to keep practising to get it right. The toast is slightly burnt, too. I prefer my toast to be yellowish brown, not brownish brown, if that makes sense."

"I will keep practising, si—Clarkskson. My apologies for the bad breakfast."

****

Akpana finished at Clarkson's home and hurried to her next client. There, she used a unique code to access the house and waited a few minutes to be joined by another colleague en route. Together, they assisted Lady Janet with a banana board to slide her from the bed into her commode chair to do number two. When she finished, they wiped her clean and assisted her with taking a shower.

"I think you need better shoes," a teammate, Rebecca, said out of the blue to Akpana. "Maybe a pair of boots or well-covered shoes for the weather and to protect your feet while doing the job."

"Where can I get good and affordable shoes?" Akpana asked. "I also need a good, padded jacket, gloves, a hat and a scarf."

"Yes, I saw you during the training and almost mentioned it. Don't worry; I'll take you to the shopping mall on our off day to buy some essentials."

Akpana was grateful. She looked forward to their outing.

The weeks went by, and things began to look good as Akpana acclimatised more to her new environment with each passing day. From her appearance, wearing a well-padded coat and a pair of long boots, she was suddenly giving off the *sisi* London (young London girl) vibes.

Akpana observed that she barely saw her next-door neighbours. She hadn't seen the person living in the room to her right since she arrived in the UK three months ago. She only heard music from the room at night, indicating that someone actually lived there. When she'd met the young man who lived to her left for the first time, they had a brief chat, and he seemed cordial. When Akpana saw the same guy in the supermarket nearby and went to say hello according to customary Nigerian fashion, he snubbed her as if he had never seen her before. It was an embarrassing moment. Had she said or done anything wrong the last time they had chatted, or had he forgotten her face? It would not be the first time she would experience such a cold attitude from someone she was beginning to see as a friend. The lovely lady who had helped her open an account at the bank did the same thing when they'd bumped into each other on the bus. She had waved at her with a smile, but the lady threw her face aside and pretended to be minding her business. Could this be a cultural practice in England, that people were only cordial when they had something to do with you at the time, and after that, it was "to your tent, oh, Israel" or did some people suffer from lousy mood swings?

She began to adopt some of these practices to save herself from many awkward moments. The lifestyle of approaching every familiar face to say hello, as her mother had taught her with heavy knocks on her head whenever she forgot to give a greeting would have to be packed up temporarily as far as living in England was concerned. She would continue to have a welcoming countenance whenever she met with a familiar face, but she wouldn't hesitate to keep it moving if the gesture wasn't reciprocated.

****

For many months in the UK, Akpana toiled in the cold winter and warm summer, moving from home to home and jumping buses to make ends meet. She encountered lovely clients in her sojourn as a caregiver, and she almost became like family to some. Some of them, like Suzzy Gibson, Alison Smith and Gary Guy, were her favourites. Suzzy always insisted that Akpana had breakfast after she was done with her care. The gesture of letting her have a cup of tea and some biscuits in her home warmed Akpana's heart and made her feel seen.

On the other hand, Alison, a renowned traveller who had had the opportunity to visit many African countries, challenged her mindset. Akpana had to be on her toes whenever she visited Alison. The lady asked questions about every place and thing and challenged Akpana to know more about her continent.

As for Gary Guy, he was a clown. "Just watch TV with me for an hour and say you did some cooking—who would tell them?" he would ask mischievously.

"Thanks, Gary. I'll just make you a quick dinner so you can take your pills," Akpana replied that day.

"Holly moly! I can make my own dinner. These people think I'm a child just because I turned eighty last year. I'm quite capable of making my meals, my lady. So, sit and let's have a cuppa while watching *Family Guy*. It is hilarious!" he said, laughing like the engine of a bulldozer.

"Shall we do it together, then?" Akpana asked to save her neck from the queries of neglecting her assigned duty, but she gave Gary the pleasure of believing in his fitness ability.

Notwithstanding these lovely encounters, some clients were unfriendly. Their speech and demeanour screamed disgust for the care workers. One time, Akpana missed her bus to the next client, and she could not walk due to the heavy rainfall. Mr Johnson wouldn't let her stay in his house for an extra ten minutes so she could catch the next bus, even though he had caused her to miss her bus. He wouldn't offer her a place in his living room to wait, nor did he ask her to leave, but his body language told her what he wanted from her at that point was to leave his house as her time with him was over. Despite the terrible weather conditions, Akpana had no choice but to wait at the bus stop in front of his house.

Running the rat race under the rain, freezing weather and snow was part of the package of working in England. Not everyone understood the struggle of earning in a country like England. Money was not plucked from trees. People laboured for it, sometimes in very harsh weather conditions, and spending wisely was an indication that the hustle was legitimate.

Being a good samaritan, Akpana found it challenging to tell people "no" whenever they made financial requests.

That attitude made it slow for her to achieve her personal goals and fuelled the idea that she was, indeed, a millionaire in the UK, earning lots of pound-sterling and sharing it on demand.

Once Akpana had offset her bills, she immediately sent her family some money for their upkeep. She attended to the school fees of her younger siblings and assisted her extended family and friends financially, too.

Bank Alert

It was a Tuesday evening in Bebuabong village. Gregory sat in his living room, holding a *Premium Times* newspaper, trying to acquaint himself with the latest happenings in the country. "These migrants fleeing the country to Europe through the desert are really endangering themselves, o," he mumbled to himself, feeling perplexed. "But many of us are prospering here in our fatherland. These young people do not want to involve themselves in agriculture, which is a very lucrative sector. They keep running away, looking for white-collar jobs by all means necessary, and if they must travel abroad, why should they go through the desert, for goodness' sake, eh? Now, look at how most of them die like chickens in the desert, all for what?" Gregory's face looked as if he had just tasted sour grapes.

"Anyways, let me close my mouth. I am not in their shoes, so I shouldn't judge them. Some people would say that we should allow the hungry man to go hunting for food. If he kills an animal, he defeats hunger. If the animal kills him, he still defeats hunger." While he was murmuring to himself, Gregory heard his Nokia 3310 cell phone beep. He picked it up, adjusting the rubber band he'd wrapped around it to keep the phone in shape and useable. With an outstretched arm to keep it away from his face, he squinted his eyes to read the message.

"Atimanu!" he called his daughter, but there was no answer. "Beyin!" he called another, but there was dead silence like before. "Adeshi! Who is there? Amokeye!" Gregory called, having lost his patience. "Too much water in the ocean and not a single drop to drink?" he said, this time feeling infuriated in the centre of his living room, wondering about the essence of having so many children who all disappeared when they were most needed.

He thought he had heard the children's voices a few minutes ago, arguing and laughing in the backyard—when had they miraculously disappeared just now-now that they couldn't hear him scream their names?

Meanwhile, in the big mud kitchen behind the house, where the cooking took place, some naughty kids were hiding in the corners, clinging to the kitchen walls to avoid being seen by their father.

"But Adeshi, you should have answered Apa. You know I have cassava to peel and wash," Atimanu said.

"Which cassava are you talking about? Same ones Ama asked all of us to join hands and do or different ones?" Adeshi asked.

"As for me, I have been running errands all day. The sun is too hot, and I am not in the mood for any message now—let Amokeye answer," Beyin said.

"Me that my tummy has been paining me since last night? Can't you see how I have been bending down like a lizard since morning?"

"All right, then. I'll answer the call. Since everybody has one problem or another, I won't feign illness for a simple errand," Atimanu said, stomping out of her father's blind spot.

"Apa!" she replied, pretending to have been gulping some water, hence her inability to respond.

"Where is everyone?" her father asked. "I just need someone to help me find my glasses. I need to read this message on my phone."

"Let me see," Atimanu said, collecting the phone from her father. "Hey! It's a credit alert."

"Credit alert? From whom?"

"From sister Akpana. She has just sent us—I mean, sent you—some money. It says here, one hundred thousand naira from Akpana Ipeh. Reason: family support."

"What did you say?" Felicia asked, jumping out of her bedroom like a frightened toad after hearing something about money. "Did you say my daughter in 'London' just sent us some pocket money?"

"Yes, Ma. The bank alert confirms that," Atimanu replied.

In her usual manner, Felicia began to dance and sing, praising God for a sign of better things to come. Ikel rushed into the living room, dancing and celebrating. When it came to money, there were rarely any enemies in sight; everyone was friends.

****

It wasn't the last time Akpana would send financial support to her family. She continued to transfer cash of varying figures monthly. One would have thought it would be the beginning of profound peace, quiet and contentment in Gregory's family, but the reverse was the case. Now and again, a fight erupted between her parents, especially because her father was fast becoming a nuisance when it came to his spending. Gregory suddenly believed he needed a brand-new motorcycle as the old one no longer looked attractive. Then, he bought new farm equipment, new pairs of trousers and shoes, spending about eighty per cent of the total money received on things that were never an issue.

"You are a useless man, Gregory Ipeh," a very upset Felicia reminded her husband, pulling the neck of his brown T-shirt tight.

"Leave my shirt, Felicia, before I do something that I will regret."

"Leave you for what reason? You, this wicked man."

"You dare abuse me, Felicia? You that I married with a very long giraffe neck? Now I have stuffed you up with so much fufu from my hard work that you now dare to insult me, your husband?"

"Which husband are you talking about, eh? So if husbands raise their hands, someone like you, Gregory, will raise a finger, too?"

"Wonderful! My eyes have finally seen my ears. So a day has come when my wife has the temerity to call me less than a man to my face? Hah! Felicia, you are fortunate I am trying to become a better man, otherwise, you would have seen pepper this afternoon for that nonsense you just vomited. Now, get out of my way before I do something that I will regret."

"You go nowhere, Gregory, until you give me some of that money Akpana sent. I also need to buy a new sewing machine. After all, you bought a new motorcycle for yourself."

"Felicia, leave my shirt alone. I do not have such money at the moment. Now, move out of my way."

"I will not move!"

"I say move, woman!"

"Force me, nau! I said I won't move an inch!"

"I have had enough, Felicia!" Gregory shouted, his soprano voice going as loud as a keyboard key. He pushed his wife to the big sofa in their living room.

Felicia let out a big scream. "Ahhhh! Ahhh! My back, o! You will not kill me, Gregory! I will not die before my time! Go and fight your mates if you think you have power!"

"I didn't hit you, Felicia, so stop making a scene."

"I will make a scene, Gregory. What do you do with the support money Akpana sends to us? Spend it on palm wine and pepper soup at Adaku's joint, carrying small-small girls old enough to be your daughters? You shameless individual!"

"Wonderful! Which money do you speak of, Felicia? That small change Akpana sends to us is what you are making a mountain of?"

"You call a monthly allowance of one hundred thousand naira a small change? How much were you earning in NRC as a salary? Eh? Answer me."

At that point, Gregory went mute. There was sadness, guilt and anger, all mixed into a display of emotions. One minute, his eyes were droopy, with his eyelids appearing heavy. Another minute, he avoided eye contact with watery eyes. The next, his fist was clenched, and he breathed hard, like one who had just run a marathon.

"Ahhh, Gregory! You hurt me badly," Felicia continued. "I have stood by you in your lowest of low. I have seen you crushed and lifted your spirit. I refused to spit on you when the world was calling for your neck from your gross misconduct at the railway. I never said a bad word about you and what you did, even if your actions cost us our home, my business, the kids' education, our friends and every comfort we were used to living in the city. And how have you repaid me? You married a small girl to spite me daily. I'm constantly on my toes because of this strange woman you brought between us, and now, you cheat me out of the money our daughter sends for our upkeep?"

Gregory looked at his wife blankly. He knew she was right, but he was determined to maintain his ego. "I do not have time for such discussions, Felicia," he said, looking away. "You keep making a mountain out of a molehill, and that is what is affecting your emotions. Maybe, when I come back, we can talk about it. For now, I have an appointment that I must attend, so *au revior*," Gregory said, shutting the door behind him.

Felicia was heartbroken. She burst into tears and wailed for a while, but she had a plan. Henceforth, she would follow her husband up accordingly, just as the famous Nigerian adage goes, "Cunny man die, cunny man bury am," which implies that a cunning man needs to be handled in a cunning way. As for her daughter in London, she would call and ask that her share of the upkeep allowance be sent directly to her bank account to avoid locking horns with her husband. She knew Akpana would oblige. After all, as most Nigerian mothers would argue, she was her mother, whom had carried her in her womb for a good nine months and breastfed her for two good years.

With the regular financial support Akpana offered at every seeming emergency, she announced herself as a renowned millionaire, doing very well for herself in England. With the culture, it was difficult to understand that one could not help a drowning man if he did not learn how to swim. The thought that Akpana financially assisted her family out of a struggling savings account or that, for many months, she'd skipped lunch, not braided her own hair, and even refrained from buying herself new items she liked because she had to make a sacrifice and send that money back home was hardly ever considered. There was always another call or text message after the last to help salvage a pressing need or two, and Akpana always obliged.

The Phone Call

It was a dark Saturday night, and Akpana had just finished a late shift. She was tired, but looked forward to a restful night for the next day's job. The new Care Is Life service user, Anna, needed a lot of care, especially before she went to bed at night. Akpana and Rebecca had assisted her in using the commode. They had wiped her clean, showered and dressed her while chatting about what Anna's days in France were like before she'd married an Englishman and moved to Britain in the seventies.

Soon, the two care workers split up their duties. Akpana assisted in preparing Anna's dinner, microwaving a pack of frozen mashed potatoes with gravy and sausages wrapped in a cling-film pack, while Rebecca did the paperwork, in which she stated every piece of information about Anna's care that night.

After Anna had eaten, the ladies called it a night, leaving the eighty-year-old Anna in her comfortable nightwear with a duvet over her chest. She watched TV happily while Akpana and Rebecca headed for the bus stop.

"See you tomorrow, Becky," Akpana said, hopping on a bus en route to her destination while Rebecca waited a few more minutes for her bus to arrive.

When Akpana got home, it was to the same quiet house she'd always come back home to with nobody to say hello or ask about her day. Regardless of her wishful thoughts, she was glad she had arrived home safely and made the sign of the cross in her usual Catholic fashion as she switched on the light bulb.

Next, she took off her Care Is Life uniform, still standing by the door entrance. She never repeated a worn uniform; they all went straight into her laundry bag after each shift, and a freshly ironed uniform was worn the next day.

She picked up the bath towel she'd left over a radiator and tied it around her chest to get ready for a shower when her phone rang. It was her mother—why would her mum call so late at night? She abandoned her trip to the bathroom and slid the green icon on her phone to the right to receive the call.

"Hello, Mummy, *kiyinah* (how is it)?" Akpana asked.

"*Kiyim kukwun ye o*! I'm not well at all," Felicia said apprehensively.

"*Kibang kiba* (what is wrong)?"

"Ah! Akpana, my own will not spoil in Jesus' name," Felicia said amidst tears. "The enemies will not unseat me from the table that the Good Lord has set before me in Jesus' name."

"Amen, Ma, amen," Akpana said anxiously, trying not to rush her mother, who kept declaring and rejecting evil arrows sent to steal her joy.

"Your brother is sick," she finally blurted. "My only son is sick, o, but the devil is a liar. He has come to kill, steal, and destroy, but my God has come to give us life and life in abundance," Felicia said, breaking down in tears.

"Easy Ama. What—"

"My enemies want to laugh at me," Felicia interrupted, "but he that is in me is greater than those in the world. Hah! Akpana, take out your rosary and begin to recite the glorious mysteries. Pray for your brother, Akpana. Begin to pray!"

"Ama, you haven't told me what happened," Akpana said.

"It's Ukwudi, o. Do you remember how he used to throw children into the fallen leaves piled up in the compound?"

"Yes, Ma, I remember well. Unimke used to love that."

"Thank you, my daughter. You still remember."

"Okay, so what went wrong?"

"Akpana, don't rush me. I'm still processing what happened."

"Sorry, Ma."

"Your cousin Ukwudi, flung Unimke into the pile as usual, and your brother slumped. He didn't come out of the pile until Ukwudi raised the alarm after five minutes of not seeing him pop out as he used to. If Ukwudi had waited one more minute, my baby would have died!"

"God forbid!" Akpana rebuked.

"Hah! The devil is a liar," Felicia continued. "He wasn't the only one who was thrown into the pile, but he was the one who slumped amongst all the children. God, why me?" she questioned.

Akpana wondered if her mother wished the predicament had befallen another child rather than her precious Unimke.

"Has he been to the hospital?" Akpana asked.

"That is where I am calling you from. Your father and Ukwudi immediately rushed him to the hospital on your dad's motorcycle. Thank God there was some fuel in the tank. With the current fuel scarcity in Nigeria, how would we have gotten your brother here on time without fuel, eh?"

"So, is he responding to treatments?" Akpana asked.

"The doctor has stabilised him, but he said his blood level is low, and he needs to be transfused as soon as possible."

"Ah, Ama—what kind of news is this? A little boy undergoing a blood transfusion?"

"What can we do, eh? Is it not a miracle that he is alive? Can we complain?"

"Madam Felicia! Madam Felicia!" Akpana heard a voice call in the phone's background.

"Yes!" Felicia responded.

"Let me call you back, Akpana. The nurse needs my attention."

"Okay, Ma."

Akpana knew that sicknesses required money. Unfortunately, she had just exhausted her income and was patiently waiting for the next month's salary. What could she do? She paced about her bedroom with her head bowed low and index finger tapping her lower lip. It was already late. She could have called her best friend, Rebecca, to assist her financially, but even if it wasn't late, she had already collected a small sum from her the previous week to assist Ama Agnes with her medical bills.

Ama Agnes had not had any relief from her waist pain for many years. The pain had escalated, causing her to be immobile. From there, she began to have other complications and was bedridden for months. Akpana had recently sent money for her medical bills, medications, and welfare. Asking for another loan from Rebecca within the same month wouldn't look good, but what could she do at a time like that?

She picked up her rosary and began to pray the 'Hail Mary'. Her anxiety caused her to fall into a deep sleep on the bare floor with a wrapped towel around her chest and her head leaning on a heap of washed clothes on the sofa, waiting to be folded.

Her phone rang noisily.

"Ah…Ama," she said, jolting back to consciousness as she answered the call anxiously.

"You are sleeping, abi? You are sleeping! Sleeping beauty! Your baby brother is sick, and we have been running around all night to find a blood donor since your dad and I were ruled out due to incompatibility, yet you sleep in your mansion in London like a baby, abi?

"No, Ma," Akpana said. "I just fell asleep while praying for him."

"So, you have the eyes to fall asleep in this dilemma? And prayer is what we will use for treatments and medications, no be so?"

"No, Ma, I didn't mean—"

"Look, let me tell you: if anything should happen to my only son, your joy will also be stolen from you, and I will hold you responsible, mark my words."

"Mum, don't say that…hello? Hello?" The line was disconnected. Akpana dropped her phone as she sank to the wooden floor, sliding along the cream-coloured wall.

What had her mother just say? That if anything happened to her younger brother her joy would also be stolen and she would hold her responsible? Why? Was she Ukwudi, the one who'd flung Unimke into the pile of leaves in the name of Jangilova—epo-motor, or was she a doctor who refused to cure her brother of his ailment? What, exactly, was her fault between 10 p.m. when the call had come in and about midnight, and what could she have done differently?

Akpana was heartbroken. She wept bitterly at that odd hour. Her mother was certainly under duress, she tried to console herself, but her words hurt like a double-edged sword. Last week, Ukwudi had asked if she wanted his mum, Ama Agnes, to die since she'd claimed she had no extra cash to send for her treatments. The pressure and guilt trip had made her borrow money from Rebecca.

That night, she was restless like the biblical King Xerxes in the book of Esther. Like the King, she began to go through her book of records. She saw that she had sent her parents their usual monthly income and supported Ama Agnes as requested. She'd also paid Amokeye's and Unimke's school fees and supported her stepmother with some money to start her new business.

Now, her pockets were bare, but perhaps they were not exhausted enough. Maybe it would satisfy her benefactors to see her collapse on the cold floor, lifeless, for her to breathe, and their lives would go on as normal. What a life, she said, sniffing into her wrapped towel.

The Revelation

Stainless and his wife, UD, had been in Lagos for almost a year. She had not applied for her Nigerian passport, let alone began her application for an American visa. For the past week, an irate Stainless had scolded her for persistently asking what was happening with their travel plans. Reality began to dawn on her, even when denial seemed more comforting.

Firstly, she noticed how overly familiar her husband was in every street in the Shogunle area in Oshodi, the same with the marketplace and the church. Still, Stainless had said this was an accommodation he had acquired temporarily until their plans to travel abroad had been hatched. Also, as soon as they had arrived in Lagos after their honeymoon, he'd begun a business she suspected had pre-existed. Had her husband been running the business through his friend, Obasi, while he was abroad? There were too many unanswered questions, and Stainless wasn't straightforward in his answers.

With a four-month-old pregnancy, UD resigned to her fate. For peace's sake, she stopped asking her husband questions about their American dream and hoped she was wrong about being scammed, but even if she wasn't, what could she do with a child on the way? She hoped her baby would be born in the US and become a citizen.

With unwavering faith that all would turn out well, UD decided to be a loving wife instead, assisting her husband in his football viewing centre, where he showed both local and international football matches on big screens for football fans. At night, she cried her eyes out, feeling sorry for herself. All her dreams of becoming a superstar were going down the drain before her eyes, and there was nothing she could do about it.

Stainless had begun to show his true colours. He'd swapped his wife's smartphone for a regular phone without an Internet connection. His excuse was that a smartphone was a distraction from attending to customers in the shop. At home, he claimed the phone was a distraction from her wifely duties. Without it, UD could no longer keep up with the usual trends on social media, and she slowly fell into depression, having nothing for herself except for the name 'UD Love', used by Stainless when he needed the warmth of his wife in the late hours of the night. That was his happy hour. When UD tried to use the opportunity to ask for all he had promised her, he simply turned his back on her and dozed off, snoring.

So, UD became her own detective, seeking answers to her bucket of questions. From her findings, she learned that her beloved sweetheart had never been to America. Although he'd planned to travel, his visa was denied due to insufficient funds to back up his trip. Since he had counted his chickens before they were hatched, he'd enjoyed a grand farewell ceremony from his village community before reaching Lagos, where his application was made and rejected, and he was too embarrassed to return home with the bad news. Like many people who would rather hide in shame than own up to their actual circumstances, Stainless simply used the little money he had to support his friend, Obasi, to pay rent for their one-bedroom apartment in the Shogunle area in Lagos while he job-hunted. Obasi had invited him over to share his one-bedroom apartment before his application was made with the hope that Stainless would not forget the good gesture and send him some cash overseas from time to time.

One cool evening, while wandering around the Oshodi Market, Stainless and his new roommate, Obasi, came across a poster under the bridge. It read, "Find the you in you." Obasi had laughed out loud after reading this ridiculous phrase, but for Stainless, the phrase had sunk deep. As an extra mouth in his friend's house, wasn't he searching for a job to help with their basic needs? Had he not been denied many job opportunities for one reason or another during his short stay in Lagos? "Oga, drop something if you want something," one man had told Stainless when he walked into his office for a job interview. Stainless knew the phrase meant that he wanted a bribe. Others had said, "Scratch my back, and I'll scratch your back," but if Stainless had the money some of the employers had requested to give him a job in their company, he would have fulfilled his main dream of being in America.

"Ubi! Close your mouth before flies come visiting your intestines," Obasi had said to his friend, who kept reading the short phrase, "Find the you, in you," his mouth agape.

"Yes! Yes! That is it, that-is-it!" exclaimed an excited Stainless, for he now knew what to do. He would work with his existing passion for football. That was when the idea of the football viewing centre was born.

Stainless had rented a shop for his business with the remaining cash initially meant for his travels. Then, he bought a used plasma television and a small generator, popularly known as I-better-pass-my-neighbour for days when there was no electricity. He got a carpenter to make eight low customer benches, four on each row, for customers to sit comfortably on while watching the game. He also got two standing fans to circulate some air during the very heated football matches, with a DSTV decoder and a subscription to view football matches. A large blackboard in front of his shop displayed the time of the various matches. As a form of entertainment, Stainless had a refrigerator to store cool drinks to be sold for extra money. Soon, other small businesses, like the small chops' sellers, began to fraternise with him in hopes of profiting from his new business.

Five years had passed in a flash since Stainless's business had commenced. He had made tremendous progress and moved from having just one plasma television to having three—with all televisions simultaneously displaying different football matches, bringing in more customers with various interests. His cemented floor was now tiled, and his standing fans had been changed to a massive air conditioner.

Then, Stainless had sought both the warmth of a wife and the cries of babies in his house. Most people believed there was barely any 'wife-material' in the big cities, so he resolved to return to Obudu, his maternal home, where he was raised by his single mother, in pursuit of a bride. What better time to do that than Christmas, when every beau returned to the village to celebrate the season with family? That was when he'd met UD, a young girl who was very ambitious, like himself. He would marry her by hook or by crook, he'd assured himself, and of course, he had.

"Ah…one chance (scam)! I don enter one chance (I have been scammed)!" UD exclaimed in a muffled tone, covering both hands over her mouth, unwilling to disturb the neighbours in the face-me-I-face-you one-room apartment they lived in. She had finally put all the puzzles together, hearing pieces of gist from neighbours, customers at the shop and some slips of tongue from her husband's best friend, Obasi, who had left his old home so the new couple could live there. He now lived in a single-room apartment in Victoria Island.

There was hardly anyone to speak to concerning her woes. She suffered from different kinds of abuse at the hands of her husband. He wouldn't even give her pocket money from the business she assisted him with, day and night. Everything she wanted had to be written down, scrutinised and approved or rejected by him. With her needs as an expectant mum being numerous, UD decided to bite the bullet by falling back to her big sister, Akpana, even though they didn't have a good relationship like most siblings. Akpana was her last resort.

UD reluctantly picked up her small pocket diary and flipped through a few pages with the phone numbers of her family and friends written down on them. Then, she saw the +44 number that belonged to Akpana. She picked up her phone and dialled the numbers nosily, after which a green button on the phone was pressed to put the call through.

Akpana's phone vibrated on the kitchen counter where it lay charging. She was sitting on the brown sofa in her shared living room in Loughborough, unsure of which programme to watch after the popular TV show *Britain's Got*

Talent. It was her day off, and she planned to have a well-rested day before her next shift. In her hand, she held the remote control, flipping through the channels. The variety of channels made it difficult for her to make up her mind on what to watch. At that point, she thought about her journey so far and appreciated life deeply while sipping her cup of tea, feeling some satisfaction within herself. Her parents and siblings were doing well in health and financially. As for UD, she must be enjoying her marriage with the love of her life, she presumed.

Just then, she heard her phone ring, and she stepped outside her thoughts. "Ah, this silly ringtone of mine. I keep saying I'll change it, but then I get too busy and forget…" Akpana continued to soliloquise as she hurried to the kitchen counter where her phone lay.

"Talk of the devil," she muttered before sliding the green button to receive the call.

"Hey, UD — it's been a while. What's up?"

"Hmmmm….Akpana, I am good." Her voice quivered as she responded.

"You are good? You sound like a frightened puppy. By the way, why are you calling me with your Nigerian number — aren't you meant to be in the US by now?"

"It's a long story, my sister." UD went through her ordeal about the stranger for a husband she now shared life with.

"No way! But I warned you, Udanshi. I told you that that guy seemed shady, just too good to be true, but you accused me of jealousy and called me all sorts of unprintable names in your usual manner. Now, you see where this has landed you?"

"I'm sorry, Akpana. I hope we can put our differences aside. I'm in a hot pot of soup, and I need your support now more than ever, especially with my condition."

"Condition? Are you pregnant?"

"Yes, sis, I am currently four months pregnant. I am stuck for life, I believe. I bragged to everyone in the village about my US trip. I looked down on my single friends and called them out of their names. How do you expect me to return home with an unborn child and a failed scam marriage in less than a year?"

"Typical UD. Always at loggerheads with people," Akpana muttered softly. "So, what's the plan?"

"All I need is some cash to start a business where I can handle and manage my finances. Please, big sis, no amount of money is too small for me."

There was a deep sense of distress mixed with a surprising element of humility in UD's voice. It was just as the biblical King David had said: "Oh, how have the mighty fallen? Tell it not in Gath, publish it not in the street of Ashkelon lest the daughters of the Philistines rejoice, lest the daughters of the uncircumcised triumph."

What a surprise it was—the bubbliest member of the Ipeh family, the life of the party, to be reduced to such a pitiful state in the twinkling of an eye. Who would have believed any human would dare stand in the way of UD's ambition to become a superstar? But life has a way of keeping one humble. UD's voracious appetite for the finer things in life was her undoing. Akpana sent an unplanned hundred pounds to assist her sister, a sum that was received with the greatest of joy.

A Fresh Start

UD woke up at cock crow to beat the strenuous Lagos traffic. Before facing the traffic, she would have to face her neighbours in the face-me-I-face-you compound she shared with nineteen other families. Since everyone was eager to beat the traffic to their business areas, places of academic learning and other places they had to be at, they all woke up early to fetch water from their shared water reservoir.

"You dey for queue?" Baba Badmus asked one young lady with a piece of wrapper around her chest, trying to jump the queue. She was a student and had an engagement to meet up with.

"Baba, abeg, I no one late, make I quickly fetch my water dey go, abeg."

"So, who one late? Go back, my friend. Next time, wake up early," yelled Madam Nkoyo, urging the young lady to respect the queue regardless of her commitment.

UD waited patiently for her turn. It was now 4.30 a.m., and she would need to join another queue to use the public bathroom, which was usually jam-packed at that time of day. To enjoy a blissful and undisturbed bath, it was best to use the bathroom from 10 a.m. onwards. That time was suitable for many jobless people roaming the neighbourhood. They stayed in there, singing all kinds of R 'n' B. In their minds, they were some sort of superstars, entertaining a crowd and getting a standing ovation. You could hear their voices squeaking like tiny rats as they strained their vocal cords, pretending to be Celine Dion.

Finally, it was UD's turn to fetch some water. She threw a bucket with a long rope attached to it into the water reservoir, scooped some water into her bucket, then made her way to the bathroom, where she waited another twenty minutes for her turn to have a quick bath before dashing to the Oshodi Market.

"Good morning, Ubi," UD murmured. She had just walked into the room after having her bath to meet her husband, yawning after his beauty sleep.

"Huh! Ubi, no more 'honey' or even 'Stainless-Bobo', as you used to call me?" he asked, half-yawning.

UD was briefly silent as she mopped her damp body with a small towel. Then, she spoke: "Is Ubi not the name that your mother and father gave to you? Please, I do not want a fight with you this morning. I have plans for the day and must dash out ASAP."

"Plans? What plans?" Stainless asked.

"Plans to provide for my baby, of course, since you are oblivious to the fact that we need to run some errands in preparation for the baby's arrival. What kind of lackadaisical behaviour is this for a first-time parent? No discussion, no antenatal registration, no shopping, nothing-nothing. Haba!"

Stainless rolled over from their Mouka foam, double bed mattress spread on the bare floor and stood on his feet, stretching his body and twisting his bones from side to side to crack them. He reached for the Close-Up toothpaste that lay on the small side table by the corner and pressed it in the middle, releasing a snake-like pepper-red paste onto his toothbrush. That angered UD more, but she decided to choose her battles wisely. Moving from pillar to post would only make her sound incoherent and cause her husband to accuse her of being hormonal.

Her gaze moved swiftly to her husband's brownish-white singlet hung on a plastic chair in their room, a few others were scattered in their wardrobe, and she had promised herself not to keep washing or putting them in order. "Do you even love me, Ubi?" she asked. "You took me out of my father's house and brought me here to suffer, living in a face-me-I-slap-you compound.'"

"Face-me-I-slap-you," Stainless mimicked with a snigger.

"If the America you promised me isn't coming forth, why can't we move out of this place to a better location here in Lagos at least, eh? Why? All my life, I have never shared a bathroom and toilet with total strangers nor queued to fetch a pale of water from a well. What kind of life did you bring me to, Ubi?"

"Oh, please! Give it a rest already. Nag, nag, nag, that's all you do. So, all the money I spent on our marriage and honeymoon came from where? Did you contribute a penny to any of the aforementioned? Do you think they move out of a place with empty pockets or travel abroad for free? Go and sit down, abeg. You thought you had found a milk cow to give you heaven on earth? Asking to go to *Big Brother Nigeria* as a married woman—would your father let your mother commit such an abomination?"

"Don't ever mention my mother in that manner, again. Don't ever!"

"Ok, madam. Sorry madam." Stainless said sarcastically, half genuflecting.

"Come off it, Ubi," UD interrupted her husband's dramatic show of remorse. "But why did you lie to me though? You know you didn't have to lie, you didn't."

"Well, I did. So?"

"My God will judge you, Ubi. Best believe I will rise above this."

Stainless let out a big roar that was annoyingly piercing to the soul. "Arise, woman. Good luck, o."

UD ignored him. She was already used to the devilish laughter and side comments her husband used to cause her pain. He seemed to enjoy it when she cried, and he burst out laughing to deepen her hurt, but not on that day. She wouldn't give him the pleasure of seeing her cry. Henceforth, she would maintain a stiff upper lip and pretend all was well within her for the sake of her unborn baby.

She quickly dressed, looking bright and cheerful, rubbed some white powder on her face and stroked some gloss on her lips.

Seeing that his wife ignored him, Stainless felt a loss of control over her emotions that fine morning. He brushed his teeth harder, like one trying to scrub dried Spirogyra from a gutter. He would probe further to understand what joy could possibly surmount his juicy jest-making.

"You still haven't told me where you are up to this early mor-mor."

"You didn't ask, did you?" UD replied.

"Hmm...Okay, now I ask: where are you going to, my beloved, lawfully wedded wife, all dressed up and sparkly?"

"Well, since you said the last time that I was a mere consumer, not bringing anything to the table to fund our dream of going abroad, I have decided to start a provision business to support our household spending and savings."

Stainless let out his jesty laughter again, mimicking his wife's voice annoyingly.

"'I have a university degree, I am a second-class upper graduate, yen, yen, yen,' only to end up as a provision seller, selling petty snacks. You see how your life has ended?" Stainless stopped between his speeches to spit out some whitish foam from his mouth into an old plastic bowl. He rinsed with water and spat into the bowl again.

"By the way, you want to announce to the world that I, your husband, am incapable of looking after my pregnant wife, don't you?"

UD was upset. Most times, she couldn't comprehend her husband's thought process. Many men would be happy that their wife was trying to be supportive of their household needs, and if they didn't want her to, they would support her needs and not leave her stranded, but not so for Stainless. One minute, he said his wife was lazy and didn't support their American dream, and another minute, he said she was trying to mock him by being ambitious.

UD stepped out of her thoughts, and she replied to him, "First of all, my life hasn't ended, Ubi, and if you care so much about what people say, you will do the needful."

"*Aha*! Now, you are speaking what I was itching to hear. So, you claim that I do not care for you, and you have resorted to stealing my money from the viewing centre to set yourself up, no be so?"

"*Ha*! Ubi. I do not handle your business money, and you know that."

"So, where did you get the money to start a business?"

UD stalled for a while. If she didn't speak the truth, her husband would likely accuse her not only of stealing but also of cheating on him. There was no way to dance around it but to come up straight. After all, Akpana was her big sister, not a stranger. "Well, my big sister, Akpana, sent me some money yesterday from England."

"Hmm…Your big sister from England sent you some money," Stainless repeated after his wife. There was a long silence in the room. It was unlike Stainless. UD expected some kind of reaction, but she'd been greeted with an odd response. She ignored him and quickly hurried to grab the bus.

Milking the Cow

The years in England seemed to fly by so quickly, it was like a sprint. Some people said it was due to the busy life the people had over there. They were in some sort of relay race of seasons. One minute it was sunny, then the baton passed swiftly to chilly days and dark clouds. The relay continued until the year ended abruptly.

What remained constant for Akpana was the strain of paying loads of bills in England while shouldering the responsibilities of her family and friends back in Nigeria. It was such a joy to hear that her father had finished paying the loan he owed the Bebuagbong community in Lagos and that he had also acquired a new piece of land to replace the one he had sold for her travels.

On the other hand, her mother had expanded her business, purchasing a big shop that accommodated many customers to sit and enjoy their meals. She now sold a variety of meals like *kiwa* (bean pudding), bread, and soft drinks, and had two shop assistants who ran errands and served customers rapidly.

As for UD, her provision business was sailing successfully. She and Stainless were also expecting their second baby and enjoying some peace between themselves with less bickering. Their joy radiated in the video calls they made to Akpana. The duo would laugh and crack jokes happily, whispering little nothings to the amusement of their observer. Who said money couldn't buy happiness? Akpana wondered on one of their video calls.

Another bit of good news was that little Amokeye was now in the university. She had recently called on the phone to excitedly inform Akpana that she'd bought the latest iPhone for herself. She asked her beneficiary to celebrate with her, as she was now one of the big girls on the school's campus.

Akpana could not believe her ears. She had never used an iPhone in her life and still managed the old phone she'd brought from Nigeria. She was shocked to her bone marrow and wondered how not-so-little Amokeye had gathered the money for such a luxury from the pocket money she sent to her, the same pocket money the young lady grumbled over because the financial support was usually not enough.

Everyone except Akpana seemed to have made headway in life. Her recipients had made tremendous progress beyond her own achievements. She survived on bank loans and credit cards and lived in debts while she sent cash to others. There were no savings in her bank account in case of an emergency. She thought hard about it and made the painful decision to cut off the money spared to her receivers. Her parents' monthly income was slashed reasonably. UD's upkeep money was stopped abruptly. Akpana believed she had helped her sister enough, especially as her business was now sailing along fine. Besides, UD had a husband whose traditional duty was to look after his wife. For Amokeye and Unimke, education was essential, and there was no way she could stop paying their school fees, or she'd open the door to the possibility of their ending up almost insignificant in society and being blamed for their lack of school funding.

These sudden decisions caused a massive friction between her and her beneficiaries. Nobody wanted the news that their free flow of cash would either be stopped or slashed. Many of her friends and family members who usually posted random pictures of her and words of praise on social media, especially on occasions like her birthday, stopped.

Stainless, a huge partaker of the monthly stipend his wife once received, seized the opportunity to cause immense strife in the heart of his brooding wife. "Who does that sister of yours think she is? She makes tons of money in the UK for doing what? Making tea and toast. Yet she stays stingy with her money. God forbids such a sister. *Tahhh!*"

"Where are you going with this?" UD asked, feeling confused by the sudden outburst.

"No, ooo. I am not going anywhere, please. Do I own a bicycle? I am here with you." He smirked.

"Come on, honey. My sister was our backbone when we needed her to be. She explained why she was no longer able to continue assisting. Even though it hurts, I thank her for the good times."

Stainless reiterated his wife's words in a funny tone. "You thank her for the good times. So that chicken feed she was sending is what you think people give their siblings from overseas? Do you know that my friend Peter, whose sister also lives in the UK, bought him a car and even built their parents a big mansion here in Lagos?"

"Honey, you are going too far with this," UD said to her husband, her left eye twitching. Her husband's words were beginning to get into her head, and she hated to believe her innermost thoughts. Seeing that he was getting somewhere with the topic, Stainless continued as if they were only having a harmless conversation.

"I'm not trying to be mean or inconsiderate, o," he said, lifting piles of books, searching for nothing in particular. "I was just wondering if it wouldn't be nice to travel to that same overseas like your sister did. After all, living in America had always been our dream."

The word 'America' hit UD like a boxer's blow. After a long time, her hopes of living in America had been revived. Her dream of being all fancy with the latest cars and a walk-in closet filled with luxurious clothes, bags and shoes began to replay in her mind. She bit her lip as her thoughts drifted to the innermost desires of her heart, which she had buried in an attempt to accept her reality.

Stainless smirked. He could see that his words had the desired effect on his wife. He feigned ignorance of the obvious and stepped out of their one-room apartment, leaving his wife's mind muddled.

****

Back in Loughborough in England, Akpana was aware of the friction her tough decisions caused the beneficiaries of her goodwill, but she stood her ground regardless and finally began to 'see' her money. She was able to gather some savings within two years of thoroughly scrutinizing every bill and being financially smart. She thought hard about a sustainable investment to put her money into. Last month, her sister UD had advised her to buy a plot of land in Ikeja in Lagos and start building her own house. The location was affordable as it belonged to the Church and was fast developing into a mega city. Akpana seemed to like the idea of owning property when she returned to Nigeria after many years of living abroad, but not a house. For now, a care company was more like her dream. She had sponsored herself in the university, where she gained a diploma in Health and Social Care, coupled with other training and CPD courses she had done over the years. She believed her experiences and qualifications would help her care business in Nigeria thrive.

More so, a re-location to Nigeria would help her get hitched. Her busy lifestyle in the country made it difficult to begin a serious relationship that could lead to marriage. Some of the men who'd approached her merely wanted to use her as a ladder to settle in the UK since she had gotten an indefinite leave to remain in the UK after her five-year work visa had expired. Also, she could never get used to the weather during the cold season. She loved that the country was peaceful, welcoming and rewarding, but she missed the presence of her people. So, she worked multiple jobs to save more money to buy a plot of land to build her own business with the help of her sister and then return home fulfilled.

Bit by bit, piece by piece, Akpana sent every penny she could lay her hands on to her sister, who had told her she bought a piece of land in Ikeja. She sent a copy of the Deed of Assignment and all related paperwork of ownership to Akpana as proof. The joy in her heart knew no bounds. She began sending hundreds of pounds over the months and years, but it was always one complaint or another. Either the price of building materials had gone up, or they had to order unique materials for the building from abroad.

Most times, Akpana paid twice and thrice for building materials because the first sets were substandard products, and they had to change them to more durable materials. On some days, UD made emergency calls, asking for more money to pay the builders to 'ginger' them to keep doing their jobs. Some builders were reported to have taken money but stopped showing up on-site, and another set of builders were hired to keep the job going. The strain of keeping up with the setbacks was a pain in the neck.

Notwithstanding, Akpana worked many extra hours to meet the task at hand. The goal was to one day return to Nigeria and run her own care business.

UD admired her sister's tenacity and applauded her effort over the phone. "My sister, my sister — if you see how your care home is coming together, ehhh...In short, I am speechless. That two-storey house you are building is actually a villa, period!"

"Villa?" Akpana asked with tickled laughter.

"Yes, nau. It's gigantic. I can't wait for you to start making money off the business. I mean, you've invested a lot," UD said.

"Of course, I will make money with time. It's a lucrative business, but for me, it's more about helping and caring for others like I have always done. You know, it's more of a passion than anything else," Akpana said.

UD didn't like Akpana's usual sermon about having a passion for people, so she rolled her eyes as her sister spoke. "Look, Akpana," UD said, "all that talk about helping people is your cup of tea. If I were you, I would build a massive house for myself instead, one that would stand taller than any house in my neighbourhood, but you chose to build a care home instead as the Mother Theresa of Nigeria. I salute you."

"UD, are we having this conversation all over again?" Akpana asked. The talk about what kind of property to invest in was long argued between the two sisters, but Akpana was firm on what she wanted.

UD gave in again. "Mmmm…let me shut my mouth and mind my business. After all, it's your money, not mine. However, you know that I will always have your back, regardless of our differences, right?"

"Right! That's exactly what I want from you: your support," Akpana said. "And I have been getting lots of that from you and my brother-in-law, Ubi, being my project supervisors. I am so thankful to you both. What else could anyone wish for in a family?"

"You are always welcome," UD said.

"By the way, I will send the money for the interlocking blocks tomorrow. Just remember to send me some pictures so I know what else to add and subtract in the care home," Akpana said.

"That's not a problem. My husband will do that when he gets to the site by the weekend," UD promised.

The rest of the evening was nostalgic. The idea of returning to Nigeria and starting her own care company one day made her heart smile. She couldn't wait to see the progress of her house. UD always sent pictures and videos from the foundation. Akpana even spoke to the site manager, who briefed her on the plan.

Although it took constant reminders, UD eventually sent a truckload of pictures. Akpana's care home was coming together nicely. Even her parents admitted they had travelled to Lagos to see things for themselves, and it was, indeed, a beautiful piece of art. She witnessed the same beauty through the pictures and videos sent to her and concluded that her care home was a slice of heaven.

A few things did, however, catch her attention. The building was coming together quite all right, but the roof colour, doors and windows differed from her requests. Also, her suggestions on the location of the toilet and bathroom to help vulnerable service users have easy access to the restroom were still pending, and she became quite upset that her orders were being flouted.

Akpana expressed her concerns about it, and UD explained why things had changed slightly from their initial arrangement.

Nonetheless, all was good, Akpana was assured. The builders would have to make a few adjustments to incorporate her requests. Besides, UD had an excellent taste, and Akpana trusted that she would take care of pending issues.

Once Upon a Christmas

It would soon be Akpana's tenth Christmas in England. She stood on the balcony of her apartment wearing an oversized red and green jumper, her gaze directed at some withered tree branches that looked thirsty and forsaken. They made her think about the close resemblance between the Harmattan season in Nigeria and the English winter, except for the heavy-laden dust the former carried in the air. The two seasons were harsh on the skin, and both had foggy and chilly days.

Lost in a maze of thought, Akpana heard a sound that made her look in the direction.

"Good morning, Joan," Akpana greeted her neighbour.

"Morning, love," Joan answered happily. Akpana smiled about how Joan referred to her as "love". she didn't know if Joan was avoiding the stress of having to call her Akpana, or if it was just one of those endearing ways the British loved to call people without any real attachment.

Joan was fixing a Santa air-pumped balloon outside her house. Weeks before, her husband Yin had climbed to their rooftop using a ladder to connect strings of Christmas lights. Other neighbours had decorated the exterior of their houses, too. Akpana believed there was a silent competition amongst her neighbours about whose house had the better Christmas decorations each year.

The house adjacent to her apartment had been decorated since October, with Christmas lights and inflated snowman air-pumped balloons dancing in their front garden. The house opposite hers had adorned the massive tree in front with colourful, shiny lights. Together, they gave the entire street a lot of festive cheer.

She admired the beauty of the night, remembering the Christmas tree she had purchased, toeing the foreign culture she now dwelt amongst. As the saying goes, "When in Rome, behave as the Romans."

As part of the celebration, some of her friends were coming over to her place, and Akpana had already put their wrapped presents under the tree.

However, she kept pondering the strangeness of Christmas trees in a home. When she was growing up in Nigeria, Christmas trees had never been a thing. At least, she didn't remember seeing one in any household. Shiny, colourful, metallic decorations and Christmas lights? Yes, there were those. They hung from one end of the house to the other, with the lights changing colours from green to blue to yellow and red and back again, with a Christmas tune playing as the lights changed consecutively.

As young girls, they wore new Cinderella dresses with matching hats and bags. She remembered that her mother would buy all their Christmas dresses as early as September or October. At that time, the price of fancy clothes and shoes was still affordable. When it got to November and December, many sellers hiked the prices due to increased demand, so Felicia bought them early at cheaper prices and hid the clothes from the kids to surprise them on Christmas morning. Upon wearing the clothes on Christmas day, a few of the kids frowned because their surprise clothes and shoes were a bit oversized, but Felicia would rather buy oversized clothes and shoes than get the sizes right. "You will grow into them, don't worry," she always said.

Young boys wore trainers. During the Holy Mass, the trainers terrorised the church when stomped hard on the floor.

"Jingle bells, jingle bells, jingle all the way…" The tune of that lovely Christmas song and others rang out from the different shoes that shone like disco lights because almost every kid wore the same exceptional designer trainers. Whenever a parent heard the Christmas tune, they looked at their kid's feet to be sure they were not one of the suspects disrupting the mass.

Many mothers wouldn't go to church on that day. They'd be with the older siblings at home, making endless batches of fried chicken. Akpana and UD were the siblings who'd stayed with Felicia to prepare their Christmas meal, while the younger ones went to church with their father.

While preparing the Christmas meal, there was usually a feud between Akpana and UD. UD hated kitchen activities. She'd rather hang around with friends, gyrating and chatting about unproductive issues. She'd complain for hours about how the pestle she used when pounding the yam was ruining her false nails or how the hot oil from the pot kept splashing and ruining her skin. So, Akpana ended up doing most of the chores after strings of arguments between the two sisters.

Almost like an open secret, the day's meals were usually fried rice, jollof rice, fried chicken and fried turkey. Pounded yam with sumptuous soups, like groundnut, egusi, beniseed or vegetable, graced the table, too, traumatising the noses of their dear neighbours as they anxiously waited for their share of the seasonal cake.

"Atimanu, Beyin, Amokeye," their mother would scream their names for the umpteenth time from their mud house firewood kitchen after the food had been prepared as they showed off their new Christmas dresses proudly. "Come and take this food to Mama Kingsley and Papa Ejima," Felicia would instruct her daughters, whose job it was to run errands after the food was prepared. For hours, they'd moved about with baskets covered with lovely white shawls, giving food to neighbours and wishing them a Merry Christmas. Many would use the opportunity to replace their food warmer bowls with the food they made, as well.

Christmas Eve was always a wild sensation. The church would be so jam-packed, with many old and new faces, especially the ones who visited the church only once a year. The latecomers sat on a bench or a white chair outside the church, with the cool Harmattan weather blowing their lips dry and the twinkling stars above looking like what had led the Wise Men to Jesus. When it clocked midnight, the church screamed at the top of their voices, "Merry Christmas!" followed by a lot of dancing and singing as everyone moved from seat to seat, wishing friends and strangers a Merry Christmas.

The way home was usually chaotic with fireworks, AKA bangers, AKA pursue-pursues, AKA knockouts, flying helter-skelter with reckless abandon. Like many parents, Gregory shielded his kids from the mayhem by spreading his arms out like a hen in an attempt to take the hit instead of his precious chicks. Other people looked for safer routes back home. Akpana was always all in for the fun and games, and she enjoyed the thrilling danger.

Christmas in England was quite different from Christmas in Nigeria. In England, for example, there was no need to break the bank for fancy Christmas clothes because who cared? Nobody saw your fancy dress anyway. Whatever was underneath your padded coat in the cold weather was your personal business. If you wanted, a Christmas jumper was perfect to get everyone in the spirit of Christmas, so there was no pressure to keep up appearances. People in England would rather spend their money on Christmas meals, decorations and gifts. The supermarkets began to stock Christmas essentials as early as September or October. People exhausted their pockets, buying and buying as the supermarket items cajoled their audience as they strolled past the aisles. Television commercials also did not help matters, broadcasting advertisements for chocolates, meal ideas, fancy gifts, and so on. At that time, new products had already been introduced into the market, packaged in the spirit of Christmas for consumers to try out. Stores also gave discounts to their customers and many people ran into debts by over-purchasing items.

On the 25th of December, nearly all the stores were closed in England except for a handful. People stayed indoors, celebrating the festivity with family and friends. This had never happened in Nigeria, where traders seized the opportunity to make even more sales. There were always massive outings, with families and lovers attending concerts and amusement parks to celebrate the birth of Jesus Christ, either in a godly way or a worldly fashion. Whichever it was, Nigerians were usually outside, but in England, it was more about family time spent indoors, exchanging gifts and having delicious dinners, than an outdoor parade of events.

"Hey, bestie!" A squeaky voice outside the door shook Akpana back to consciousness.

"Rebecca is here," Akpana said walking briskly to the front door. "Look who arrived first! Becky of London. Any other Rebecca in the whole of London is just a wannabe. Tell them I said so."

Rebecca's squeaky voice let out mouse-like laughter. "You know how to wind me up, don't you? Move aside and let me come in. It's rude to leave your guest hanging by the door."

"What's all this you have with you?" Akpana asked as Rebecca shuffled in, carrying oversized packages—a bottle of rosé wine, some wrapped gifts, home-cooked jollof rice, and grilled chicken—in a big carrier bag.

"Oh, Rebecca, all this for the party?" Akpana asked, marvelling at the items as Rebecca offloaded them onto her kitchen counter. "I appreciate this, love. Please sit while we wait for Johnnie and co."

Just then, there was a bang at the door. For a second, the two ladies nearly took shelter for fear of it being a natural disaster, but it wasn't a disaster trying to pull down the entire house. It was big Johnnie, banging on the door like it was no man's business.

"Oh, my goodness! You're going to break my door, Johnnie!" Akpana exclaimed while letting her guest in.

"Akpans! Kpans! The Kpana's kpan!" Johnnie teased.

"Big head," Akpana said, hitting Johnnie slightly on his cheek. "Stop playing with my name."

"Come here, my little pumpkin pie." Big Johnnie grabbed his friend in a warm embrace. "I hope you have lots of food here because I am starving already."

"Typical Johnnie. Come in, *jor* (please). You haven't stepped in yet, and you are already requesting food, Mr. Foodie," Rebecca remarked playfully, standing up to hug him.

"Becky of London. Accurate timekeeper. Am I surprised you are the first to show up? Nope!" Johnnie roared with laughter as Rebecca walked up to greet him.

"Ahhhh…Becky, I'm mad at you," Johnnie said.

"Here we go again," Becky muttered. "What is it this time?"

"You dumped us here in the East Midlands for a new life in London—is that fair? I thought friends were meant to stick together in thick and thin."

"Come on, Johnnie. Change is constant," Akpana interjected. "Besides, have you heard that Becky is now the manager of a care company in London?"

"Ahhhh…Becky—small girl doing big things." Big Johnnie screamed as he cantered around the house excitedly. "Mad, o…doings is plenty. So why didn't you gist me about this great news? Eh, Becky? It's not fair, o. We used to be five and six back in our days in the Care Is Life company."

"Johnnie, calm down, jor," Rebecca said. "We'll talk about all of that, don't worry."

"Okay, guys. From the look of things, we have a lot to catch up on, but there is time for all of that, so let's take it one step at a time. We've got all weekend. No rush," Akpana said.

It wasn't long after Rebecca and Johnnie returned to the big blanket seat Akpana had spread on her carpeted floor for her guests that Emeka, Kim and Bisi joined the group. They were like one big, happy family in their home away from home. All of Akpana's friends were Nigerian except for Kim, a British girl from Leicester who had also once worked in the CIL company.

The first thing the guests did before sitting was to drop their wrapped gifts under the tree until it was 00.00 a.m. on the 25th of December. They sat in a big circle by the nicely decorated Christmas tree and chatted about everything and all sorts. What they said was almost impossible to hear as everyone talked over everyone else. At some point, Akpana, as the host, had to call for some order, and they all agreed that when someone spoke, the others must wait their turn to speak and not interrupt. They discussed their plans for the future and the following summer holiday itinerary. Rebecca told them about her new job and all the responsibilities that came with it, while Akpana talked about leaving England after she had saved enough money. When she got to Nigeria, she would begin to scout for the elderly whose families were far away or busy with work and didn't have time to care for them. They would be well looked after by her staff in her care home which her sister was helping her put together, she bragged.

"Wow! I can't believe you want to care for people as a full-time profession. I thought you just did it for the money," Kim said, amazed.

"Kim, you sound like you don't know Akpana. She is the queen mother of the world, always carrying people's problems on her shoulders," Bisi, a young Yoruba lady from Western-Nigeria, said with choking laughter.

"Come to think of it, have you been home yet to see how the building is going?" Emeka, an Igbo colleague from Eastern-Nigeria, asked his host.

"Well, not exactly. My sister is managing the project for me, and I trust her judgement. Besides, she feeds me with pictures and regular videos on how things are going."

"That sounds great, but I think you should also visit to see things for yourself and make certain adjustments to your taste, don't you think so?" Emeka asked.

Akpana nodded as he spoke, his words striking different chords in her mind. She never really thought of things that way. A quick visit back home after all these years would be fabulous. Her initial plan was to gather enough money from working hard and then relocate home permanently, but what harm would it do if she went a bit earlier?

"Enough of the talking, guys. We need to check the time for the countdown to Christmas," Johnnie said, opening the YouTube app on his tablet. "Oh, yeah. Just in time. About fifteen seconds to go. Countdown from ten, everyone!"

"Ten, nine, eight, seven, six, five, four, three, two, one, zero…….Merry Christmas!" the group of friends screamed out their lungs, excitedly jumping, waving, clapping and sipping wine. Rebecca led a prayer, thanking God for the gift of our Lord Jesus Christ, who was the reason for the season. Pieces of chicken followed as glasses of wine clinked, and then they unwrapped their Christmas presents.

Akpana received some makeup kits, sneakers, a purse, a set of lingerie, and a nice scarf. The others all had a gift from each person in the room, so everyone received at least five gifts each. They all fell asleep on the big blanket like one happy family. It took Akpana longer to drift to sleep as she pondered the idea of a prompt visit to Nigeria.

Home At Last

It was a very sunny day in Lagos, and the flight had just successfully landed at the Murtala Muhammed Airport. Some passengers mumbled a quick prayer, thanking God for journey mercies. Akpana made her way out of the plane with her hand luggage. She entered the airport and waited to collect two very huge boxes. In the boxes were clothes, souvenirs, and raw food items like pasta, tea bags, tomato puree and chocolate bars for members of her huge family, who would be glad to receive these 'abroad' items. Food items from abroad automatically tasted better, and the clothes would presumably last longer than the ones made locally in Nigeria.

Akpana approached a taxi driver to take her to UD's address, which she'd received from their sister Beyin. She planned to surprise UD with a visit and then return to her hotel room on Lagos Island.

She was still putting her boxes together when the driver said aggressively, "Your money na thirty thousand naira."

"That's ridiculous, sir. I do not have thirty. Please, take twenty."

"Madam, you dey waste my time, abeg," the driver replied, pretending to walk off. At that point, the whole game of bargaining dawned on Akpana. First, she spoke the 'Queen's English' and needed to quickly switch to Nigerian pidgin or risk portraying herself as a Jonny-just-come (newbie). Besides, was she not born and brought up in Lagos? She also had to pretend to be uninterested by hiding her desperation to get out of the scorching sun, so she picked up her bags and pretended to walk off.

Seeing that she wouldn't budge, the driver gave up on the game. "Oya, bring twenty-eight-K."

"Oga, I no get, abeg. Take twenty-five."

"Okay. Bring twenty-six. Just add one-K on top."

"Oga, twenty-five or nothing."

"Okay, twenty-five thousand, five hundred naira. Make we leave am like that. Just because I like you, o, no be say e pay me." The elderly driver began to pack her luggage into his boot before she could agree to the additional five hundred naira, but it was okay. Besides, she had budgeted thirty thousand Naira for the journey, so twenty-five thousand, five hundred Naira was a good bargain.

The ride home was chaotic, with a lot of cars honking and a lot of shouting and swearing from one angry driver to another. Akpana was not sure whom to give attention to: the chatterbox driver, who kept talking about his family woes without being asked, or the street hawkers screaming into her ears to purchase their goods. There was a brief traffic jam, so she wound down her car window and succumbed to a few hawkers and bought a La Casera soft drink and her favourite sausage roll, Gala. She looked at the banana hawker, trying to poke her eyes with her juicy, ripe bananas, but she simply turned away. She could never forget her vomiting incident back in the day when she'd spilt banana and groundnut puke on her fellow passengers. She quickly wound up the car window to lessen the external noise while enjoying her chilled La Casera drink in the hot car without air conditioning, nodding her head to the Afro beat music on the radio.

"We don reach the place, madam," the driver said to Akpana as he pulled over to the side of a big white and grey two-storey building. The gate was massive and well-decorated, just like the rich homes seen in Nollywood movies. Akpana began to wonder if they were at the right house, but the driver was adamant he had the location right and that he was familiar with the area, so Akpana finally succumbed to his persistence. She briefly left her luggage in the boot of the car to confirm he was right.

A white Mercedes Benz pulled out from the house just before she could knock on the gate. The driver was a lady, who wound down the car window. She looked shocked. Were her eyes deceiving her, or had she just seen a ghost?

Akpana let out a big scream: "UD, baby! The one and only Mrs Ubi. The finest! The cutest! Oh, my days! Just look at you, looking fly and all that."

UD managed a smile. Still in shock, her left eye twitched frantically. "Akpana! Is this your face?"

"What do you mean by is this my face? Do I have plastic on?"

UD chuckled gently. "Not that, but you look fresher since last I saw you."

"Of course, nau. Who goes to the Queen's country and returns the same?"

The two sisters laughed.

"What a pleasant surprise. I was going to do my hair, but I would have to cancel my appointment for another day. My sister is back, and we will paint the town red," UD replied.

The sisters walked into the humongous house, seemingly belonging to the Ubis, with the gateman pulling Akpana's luggage behind them.

The house's exterior was only the tip of the iceberg compared to the interior setup. There was a long staircase running from top to bottom in a slanted fashion. In a different segment of the house was a massive dining table covered with a creamy silk table cover, running from one end to the other. Freshly plucked flowers in vases had been placed strategically on the table, giving the dining area a fresh elegance. Almost touching the flowers was a low-dropping silver chandelier adorned with crystals. Its bulbs were lit, so it would shine its way to the hearts of admirers. Anyone who saw the house's interior would agree that money was good, indeed.

Akpana's mouth gaped in astonishment. "UD, don't tell me you bought a whole house without informing me."

"Ahh forget this, sis. I was going to inform you, but the stress from daily struggles kept taking it off my mind."

"Nope! I'm not buying that, sisi. We talked almost daily, and you didn't find a way to share this good news? Or maybe you didn't want me to steal your deco ideas, abi?"

The two sisters laughed briefly, with UD's eyes twitching uncontrollably.

"Well, congrats on your house. This is very impressive. Even if I'm still unhappy, you hid it from me. It's too early to start our usual fights, right?" The sisters laughed again.

"Please, I need to see the care home before it gets dark so I can sleep well tonight."

"Come on, sis—it's getting late, and you need to eat some food, have a bath and rest. We will do that tomorrow."

"But it's just 3 p.m.," Akpana protested. "Besides, I had some snacks on my way here. I need to see how far things have gone to sleep well. Please."

UD objected once again. Before leaving the house, her sister must eat and rest well. She also texted her husband about Akpana's sudden visit to Nigeria.

Stainless rushed quickly home from the Ikoyi Golf Club he had recently joined to mingle with those who mattered and feel like a big boy in Lagos. He seemed delighted to see his sister-in-law and offered her a special bottle of wine as the good brother-in-law he was.

Akpana could not reject the gift, even though her tummy was filled with food that had been nicely prepared by UD's maid. She had a few sips and found herself in a faraway dreamland.

Stainless lifted his tired sister-in-law, helped her to the guest room and returned to his bedroom for a confab with his wife.

"We need to do something and do it fast," a panicked UD said to her husband while pacing up and down in their spacious bedroom.

"But I thought she wasn't coming back until after two years or so. What is she doing here now?"

"Ask me again, Ubi. Ask me again, o…" UD sat on the edge of the bed and got up again restlessly. Even with the air conditioner on, the duo was sweating like two Christmas goats approaching a slaughterhouse.

Stainless dropped a bomb: "We must take her out."

"Eh? Take who out? My sister?"

"Yes. It's our only way out. Especially because she didn't tell anyone that she was coming to our house."

"No way! There must be another way. She is my blood sister, for crying out loud."

"You didn't think of that when you diverted her project money into your personal bank accounts and presented her with evidence of a two-storey school building, claiming it was her care home, did you?"

"Enough, Ubi! Did I do any of that on my own? Were you not the one who masterminded the whole thing from the get-go? Were you not the one who paid the site manager to let us record the premises and even doctored many photos and videos to suit the narrative that was sent to my sister as evidence? Eh? Answer me, Saint Ubi!"

Stainless grabbed his wife around her waist. He held her chubby face and gave her deep kiss on the lips. "UD, love," he said, his eyes appearing dreamy and his voice as cool as the early morning stream. "This fight we are trying to start will not get us out of this situation. I drugged your sister with some heavy sleeping pills, knocking her out, but we must use this opportunity to leave this house tonight with every valuable item of ours that can be carried easily. Either that, or we kill her."

"No, no killing, please. I shall prepare my bags and that of the kids. Just think of the next step while I get ready."

****

It was 12.35 p.m. the next day when Akpana woke up from a strange sleep. She vividly remembered that it had been about 5 p.m. when her brother-in-law had arrived at the house the previous day. They'd had a quick catch-up, and that was the last thing she remembered. She stretched and yawned widely, trying to make sense of having such a deep sleep. She looked at her outfit and was shocked to see that she had slept in her travel clothes. How could she have slept for so long? She may have been exhausted from the journey, especially after the terrible Lagos traffic from the day before, but the sudden doze-off seemed questionable to her. UD should have some answers, she thought.

She tried to get up, but a massive headache knocked her back into bed. She managed to maintain some composure and found her way out of the room.

"UD!" she called out to her sister. "Udanshi, Where are you?"

There was no reply.

Just then, one of the staff approached Akpana. "Where is your madam?" Akpana asked.

"She and oga don comot since last night."

"Last night, you said?"

"Yes, madam, with big-big travelling bags, like they want to travel."

"Travel? Travel to where?" Akpana decided not to give much thought to what the young staff member had said. She freshened up, had a hot meal, and called her sister's mobile number. An automated reply came from the handset: "The number you have dialled is switched off; please try again later." She kept dialling the phone number, but the response was the same.

She called her brother-in-law to find out where they were but received a similar automated reply: "The number you have dialled is not reachable at the moment; please try again later."

Akpana was confused. She would have to inform the police about their sudden disappearance. *Who left their house when they had a guest around*, she wondered.

The search continued for weeks, with the Nigerian Police involved. They assured Akpana that the couple was safe and had deliberately left their home, based on their investigation. They asked that she gave them time to gather more information.

Akpana was overwhelmed by the events when her long-time friend, Odette, came around to provide her support. They both talked about old memories that made them cackle like little children until they remembered the situation at hand, and Akpana began to weep again. Together, they held hands and prayed that all would be well and that UD, Stainless and their kids would return home safely.

Later that day, Odette asked that they visit her care home for the first time to ensure the project was sailing along smoothly in the absence of the project's supervisors. It would also do Akpana some good to have a look around Lagos, or she might get depressed, locked up at home and crying over her sister's disappearance.

"Do you have the documents for the property?" Odette asked. "At least that would confirm to the site manager that you own the property."

"Yes, I do," Akpana said, reaching for hard copies of the land and building documents her sister had emailed to her. She and Odette journeyed in Odette's blue Toyota Camry to Ikeja where the care home was said to be situated.

A lot of things had changed in Lagos, and Odette wanted to be sure Akpana had noticed. "Did you notice that buses now stopped at bus stops only to pick up passengers and not stopping carelessly wherever they saw a flag-down as they used to do?" Odette asked, nodding her head to the afrobeat music from her car.

"Really?" Akpana asked, not having noticed any change as she never had the chance to explore the city while she lived there.

"Did you also notice that roads are brighter and spacious? Most of the market men and women who sold their goods by the roadside have been banned from doing so by the government," Odette said.

"Wow! But they are just poor people trying to make ends meet," Akpana argued. "The business they do, although by the roadside, takes many sellers off the streets where they would have been a nuisance and causing mischief about the place."

"Well, you are right about that, but selling by the roadside the way most of them did was detrimental to their lives and that of others, and also it made the place look disorganised," Odette replied.

"Anyways as long as the government gets them a better place, it won't be too bad, but displacing people without an alternative? That would be disastrous," Akpana said.

"Okay, o. Here we are. Your care home should be around here somewhere," Odette said, indicating that her car was about to turn right.

"Are you sure?" Akpana asked, barely seeing a new house in sight. "Maybe we should ask some of the dwellers here, and they can direct us properly," Odette replied.

Soon, an elderly man walked past them. He was dressed in a green traditional Yoruba attire—an *agbada*, he had a chewing stick stuck in his mouth and spat out some bits occasionally. Odette quickly turned off her car engine and saluted the elder, bowing her head slightly to show some respect.

"Good morning, baba. Please, we are looking for this address," Odette said, showing the address on the document to him.

He pulled his glasses downward and stared at both the document and the handler for a while. "Which of you owns this property?" he asked.

"It's me, sir," Akpana replied from the passenger's seat in the car.

"Okay. You can park your car somewhere there and come with me. I will take you to the place," he said, pointing to a parking spot in a residential area.

Akpana and Odette came out of the car and took a long walk with the baba, enduring his slow pace and filling in some of the silence between them with small talk.

"This is the place," the baba said, pointing to a deserted plot of land surrounded by long grass and abandoned refuse the villagers had dumped.

"It's the wrong location, baba. Maybe we can check another place," Odette said.

"It's not the wrong place, my daughter. All the lands in this area are under my care. That is why when I saw the documents, it piqued my interest. This land here is for one church like that. They always come here for fasting and prayers."

"No, baba, no. I insist you check again," Akpana said with sweaty palms and a big twist in her stomach that felt like diarrhoea.

"Ah..Ah...young girl, you want to teach me about a village that I have been managing for over ten years now? Do you now claim to be more knowledgeable than myself?" the upset baba asked in a thick Yoruba accent.

"Ah... *rara o*. Not at all, sir. Thank you so much for your help, *ese*, sir," Odette said, appeasing the upset man, partly in Yoruba.

"Let me take a look at those documents again," the baba said, having calmed down. "Ah-ah, but these documents are fake nau," he exclaimed.

"Fake? Rara o. This is my property, sir. My younger sister bought it for me, and these are the documents," Akpana replied, trembling.

"Ah...you must be very naive. Even my little grandson can tell that these documents are as fake as fake can be. Look at the stamp used and look at the uncoordinated signatures of the same person that signed all documents — they don't match!"

It didn't take long before the community began to gather. They all agreed that the address tallied with the area, but there was no new development in the vicinity. Akpana felt helpless. She looked around dazed and confused.

Reality dawned on her slowly but surely. She had been duped by her own family.

"No wonder! No wonder! No wonder!" she exclaimed loudly, bringing her hands to her head and pacing about the place. She thought about the clues she should have seen but chose to ignore.

"I am a fool! Odette, what did I say? I said I am the biggest fool of the century. Ah…Ah…Ah…Ah!" Akpana screamed.

Sympathisers rushed to console her, but no amount of persuasion could calm her down as she collapsed on the sandy floor weeping bitterly.

She felt betrayed, manipulated and exploited. Thoughts of her sleepless nights, working extra shifts and multiple jobs in the snow, rain and sun flashed through her mind, and she wailed inconsolably. All her years of labour, and there was nothing to show for it.

An Adversity

Back in Bebuagbong village, members of the Ipeh family gathered in the village Town Hall, whispering in small groups and shaking their heads indiscriminately. A small calabash with kola nuts and a keg of freshly tapped palm wine had been left on a table in front of the gathering. Gregory said a quick prayer: "Like our people say, kola nut is life — may these kola nuts bring us good health, happiness and peace of mind."

Voices chorused, "*Whuo kongigbeb* (You've spoken well)."

"And may this palm wine unite us as a family as we savour its tastiness."

"Whuo kongigbeb," they all responded.

Gregory broke the kola nuts into small pieces to be passed around. Then, he picked up a small calabash cup and poured some palm wine from the keg. A bit of the wine was poured on the floor as if he were making a libation, feeding the gods, but not exactly; sometimes, insects got trapped in the tasty wine and had to be poured out. He emptied the cup of wine into his mouth, squeezed his face at the tangy taste, and opened his mouth wide, exclaiming, "Ahhhhhhh!"

In traditional Bette settings and in many Nigerian cultures, people tasted drink and food in the presence of their guests before serving them. It was a way of establishing trust by showing the drink was not poisoned and was safe for drinking.

Utsu, the first son of Gregory and Ikel, helped pour the keg of palm wine into calabash cups held by their owners and waiting to be filled. When the cup was filled with palm wine, the guest said, "k*ikpe, woshior* (That's enough, thank you)".

The guests chewed their kola nuts happily, making crunching sounds as they relished the bitterness of the nuts on their tongues and the sweet aftertaste down their throats. The fresh palm wine was a great drink to wash down the nut, and people seemed pleased with their refreshments.

"Utsu, is now a big boy o," one elder said. "Look at his strong arms, lifting the keg of palm wine like a big man."

"Don't you know that children these days grow like agric fowl," another elder remarked playfully.

Gregory returned to his bamboo recliner chair and watched the events with folded arms. The gathering reminded him of his presence in the Yaba Chief Magistrate Court many years ago. Only this time, the transgressor was his daughter. As Ukandi Emma, his older brother, stood to speak on matters on the ground, he remembered Judge Damian Okoro in the creamy-coloured courtroom, reading from a book as he gave his verdict. To mask his anxiety, Gregory shook his spread-out legs rapidly, jiggling the loose wrapper between his thighs.

Felicia sat in the corner with her face buried in her wrapper. She sobbed quietly, blowing a string of mucus from her nose into an old piece of wrapper she had been using as a handkerchief.

Ikel had her hand on her cheek with a mountainous pregnancy sitting between her thighs. She sighed occasionally and patted Felicia's shoulders in consolation.

Akpana had arrived home after ten years abroad, but the day, which should have been met with a grand celebration, was like a burial ceremony.

"You are welcome, our beloved daughter," Ukandi Emma spoke. "We are happy you returned to us in one piece from the white man's land after many years."

"Thank you, sir," Akpana replied.

"Also, you didn't go there and forget your roots. We received phone calls and gifts from you occasionally, especially during the festive seasons. Most of all, thank you so much for your assistance towards your aunt's medical bills. You were relentless in your financial assistance, and may God continue replenishing your pockets."

"Amen, sir," Akpana said softly.

"Although we all fought tooth and nail for my beloved sister Agnes to survive her illness, God knows best, and in all, we give him thanks." Ukandi Emma paused, biting his lower lip sadly. "May the soul of our beloved sister Agnes, who has gone to be with the Lord through the mercies of God, rest in perfect peace."

"Amen!" they all chorused.

"Now, to the matter at hand. What happened between you and your blood sister is very unfortunate, to put it lightly. It got me thinking of what my grandfather used to say when we were younger. He used to say: 'If a crocodile could eat its own eggs, what, then, would it do to the flesh of a frog?'"

"*Owe* (Right)!" voices concurred.

"All attempts to reach Udanshi and that devilish husband of hers — Stainless, or whatever — have proven futile. I sent Barrister Donatus, who resides in Lagos, to help us enquire about their whereabouts, but the news I received this morning wasn't good at all."

There was a lot of agitation on the faces of the people. What could the bad news be? Had they been kidnapped as those refusing to accept UD's madness believed? Were they stranded somewhere without assistance? The people kept their questions to themselves, not trying to rush the elder, yet their eyes showed an eagerness for him to speak up.

Ukandi Emma broke the news: "I know this might be a shocker to all of you, but Udanshi and her family are currently in the US as we speak."

"*Jesu!*" voices from the corners screamed.

"It is finished," they concluded.

"A friend at the Immigration Office gave Barrister Donatus this information in confidence. The house they built for themselves, which I hoped you would reclaim, was built in the name of Stainless's mother, so the house is technically hers. I am very sorry, my child, but there is hardly anything to be done at this point. Barrister Donatus has agreed to represent you in court so that you can claim the house at least. Although, it might take many years of going in and out of court, but there is hope you might succeed."

Akpana uttered a muffled cry from a lost voice that had been wailing for weeks. Odette immediately pressed her friend's head to her bosom, seeing the effect of the finality of the news. They both hoped there had been a bit of misunderstanding somewhere that needed clarity.

Felicia rushed to offer her daughter some support, but she shrugged her off, screaming, "Leave me alone!"

"You and Apa had assured me that my project was sailing fine and everything was going as planned. It was your assurance that gave me the confidence to keep sending funds to Udanshi despite my knowledge of her mischief. Did you and Apa actually see the house? Did you?"

"I am sorry, my daughter. Please forgive us," Felicia said tearily. "When we went to the site, it was deserted, but UD assured us that she would begin the project in no time. She made us promise not to tell you otherwise. I called every day, warning her to start building the house, which she told us she had, but because we couldn't continue to travel to Lagos frequently, we took her word for it. I admit I was careless, but I didn't think UD would cause you any harm. Please, forgive her, my daughter; she is still your blood, your sister."

"My blood sister? That good-for-nothing, greedy child of yours ceases to be my sister!"

"Ah — don't say that. You cannot throw the baby and the bath water away. Please, my dear. She is still your sister. Forgive and forget," Felicia begged.

"Forgive and forget? Ama, do you have a clue how much money, time and thoughts I put into my investment while still running helter-skelter to meet up with the insatiable demands from all of you? No, ma, I bet you don't, because you people believed that I plucked my money from short trees on the streets of England rather than sheer handwork. For forgiveness, that would never happen, but forgetting, yes! I will forget all of you. Delete you all from my memory, like you never existed," Akpana said.

Odette whispered something in Akpana's ear, but she pulled her head away from the warmth of the lips that gave counsel.

"Let me speak, Odette! Let me speak my mind for once! All of them sucked me dry with their endless financial demands. Their needs were insatiable. I just couldn't please any of them with all I did. They exploited me, played on my emotions, and milked me dry whenever they deemed fit. I was only as good as the last assistance I rendered, but I kept shut and accepted my cross. Then I made a small request about something as delicate as my life's project, and you see how useful they all became to me. You see?" Akpana said with a cracking voice.

"Don't talk like that, my child. I know you are upset but we can settle this amicably," Gregory chipped in unconvincingly. His mouth spewed hope, but his countenance had accepted defeat.

Akpana stood up from the stool she had sat on and made her way to the centre of the round circle. Odette jumped up to follow her as she had done since the incident at the supposed building site, jumping up to follow Akpana whenever she wandered off absent-minded. She feared Akpana might hurt herself, but Akpana beckoned for her friend to take a seat.

"I greet you all, my elders and family," Akpana said.

"We greet you, too," they responded.

"I sincerely apologise for my irrational reaction to what has befallen me. Many of you that know me, would remember that while I lived here with you from my teenage years, I tried to behave myself, being respectful, loving and selfless. So, I beg that you pardon my emotions which I have absolutely no control over at the worst time of my life.

Today, I stand before you as Akpana Ipeh, clothed yet bare, full of life yet empty, present yet lost in a maze of anger, regrets and wishful thinking. Regardless of that, I know that better days are yet to come, so I stay hopeful.

I may one day forgive my offenders, but I shall forsake them all.

With that, I say on this day, with heaven and earth bearing me witness, as I step my foot outside this village, I shall never return in good or bad. Though it tarries, I shall get back on my feet again."

With that, Akpana took her passport and left for England empty-handed. She never called back home, nor did she step foot inside her family compound again.

Gregory's Family

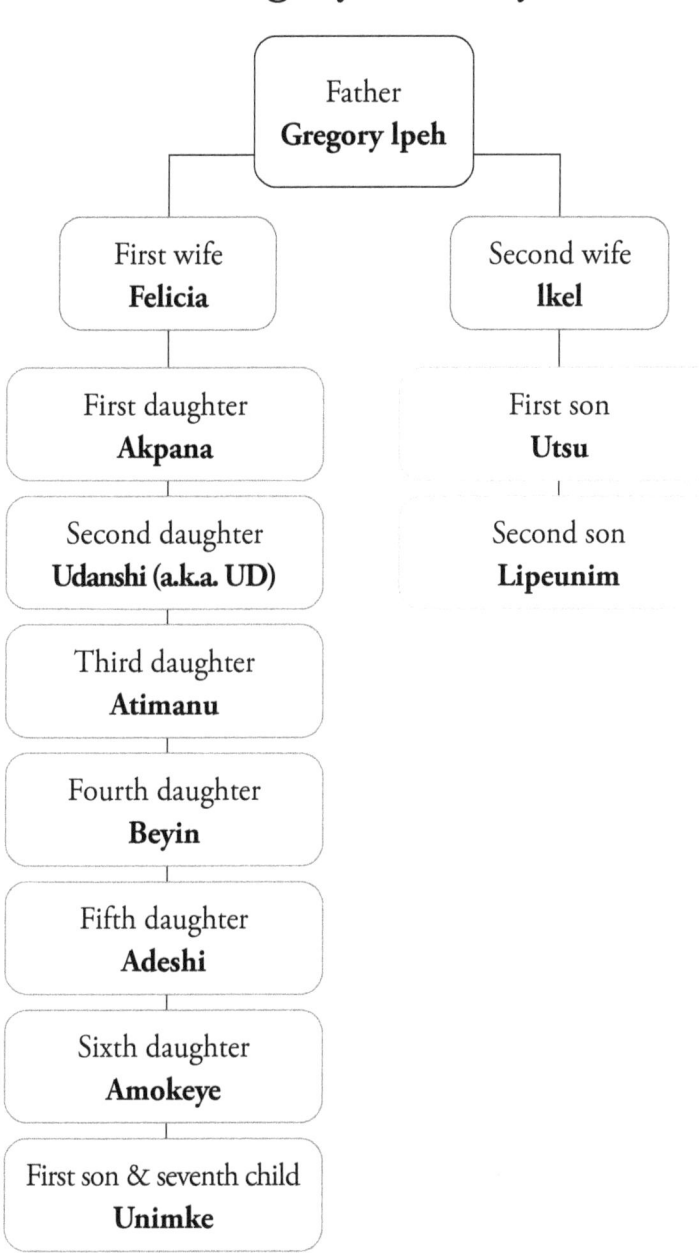

- **Father: Gregory Ipeh**
  - **First wife: Felicia**
    - First daughter: **Akpana**
    - Second daughter: **Udanshi (a.k.a. UD)**
    - Third daughter: **Atimanu**
    - Fourth daughter: **Beyin**
    - Fifth daughter: **Adeshi**
    - Sixth daughter: **Amokeye**
    - First son & seventh child: **Unimke**
  - **Second wife: Ikel**
    - First son: **Utsu**
    - Second son: **Lipeunim**

Acknowledgments

My journey to bringing this piece of art to life was backed up by a chain of support system to whom I am forever grateful for their unwavering support, encouragement, and love.

First, to my maker-God Almighty; for his grace and mercies in helping me achieve my dream of publishing this novel.

To my darling husband, Justin Udie, Ph.D. Who was my biggest cheerleader and critique.

Although the pangs of his criticism knocked me off a few times, they all came together in putting this book to shape.

To my parents Mr Kinu and Mrs Mary Undiandeye, who bought me books at a young age and have been very eager to see what I have been writing.

To my children, who have felt inspired to one day write a story and have encouraged me throughout this process.

To my favourite writer Buchi Emecheta, who made me fall in love with reading books and whose style of story telling has shaped my writing abilities.

To Conscious Dreams Publishing for their hard work and dedication in bringing my book to life.

And to several friends and acquaintances whose eyes glowed when I mentioned that I was writing a book.

I appreciate you all.

Conscious Dreams
PUBLISHING

Transforming diverse writers
into successful published authors

www.consciousdreamspublishing.com

authors@consciousdreamspublishing.com

Let's connect

www.ingramcontent.com/pod-product-compliance
Ingram Content Group UK Ltd.
Pitfield, Milton Keynes, MK11 3LW, UK
UKHW031031161224
452563UK00004BA/152